Butterfly Farm

Grace Foster

"We delight in the beauty of the butterfly, but rarely admit the changes it has gone through to achieve that beauty."

Maya Angelou

C O N T E N T

Chapter one 7

Chapter two..............................16

Chapter three...........................24

Chapter four............................27

Chapter five............................31

Chapter six...............................38

Chapter seven.........................44

Chapter eight..........................54

Chapter nine...........................63

Chapter ten..............................72

Chapter eleven...........................82

Chapter twelve...........................95

Chapter thirteen.....................…......102

Chapter fourteen.......................107

Chapter fifteen..........................113

Chapter sixteen.......................…...127

Chapter seventeen.....................…...133

Chapter eighteen.......................139

Chapter nineteen.......................149

Chapter twenty.......................…...154

Chapter twenty-one....................162

Chapter twenty-two....................171

Chapter twenty-three..................…...178

Chapter twenty-four..........…..........183

Chapter twenty-five....................191

Chapter twenty-six.........................195

Chapter twenty-seven.....................202

Chapter twenty-eight......................207

Chapter twenty-nine.......................222

Chapter thirty..............................234

Chapter thirty-one........................250

Chapter thirty- two........................262

Epilogue....................................271

ACKNOWLEDGMENTS

This book is dedicated to my wonderful family and all of the unsung heroes who work to save our planet- thank you.

Chapter one

The overhead train hummed along the tracks as it weaved its way to Tooting Bec. Katherine Reynolds unfastened one of the buttons on her Valentino blazer and sank back in her seat, looking forward to a hot bath and a cold gin and tonic. She decided to do a quick deep breathing exercise, which she knew defeated the point of it. She focussed on the rise and fall of her chest, trying not to think about what had happened at work. She wanted to avoid getting caught up in a negative thought loop but it was almost impossible, what with the lights of the city racing past her window.

At that moment, she caught sight of herself in the glass. For a thirty-five-year-old she looked tired and washed out. That was the price of 'having it all' she thought, wryly.

"Katie! Katie. Didn't realise you were on this one." Lucy thumped down onto the seat next to her, forcing Katie to shuffle over and sit up straight.

"Thought I'd missed you." Lucy was like a force of
nature and never failed to give Katie an energy boost.
"No, had some witness statements to sign off on
before tomorrow. Court deadline."
"Oh, I know, very stressful." Lucy said almost
dismissively.
But the fact was that Lucy didn't know. Lucy worked
in an events company which made the wellbeing of
their staff a core principal. They did things like Secret
Santa and lunchtime yoga. Katie, for her part, worked
in a seemingly toxic, male heavy, tier-one law firm.
She was however lining herself up to make Partner on
the next round of promotions.
She expected to hear by the end of the month.
"Did that new environmental lawyer move into your
house share? "Katie asked. She was too tired to care
but knew that she needed to make the effort.
"Yes," Lucy raised her eyebrows to suggest a fresh
development in the story and lent in conspiratorially
"Daniel Beardsley is his name. And, yes, he is as
hairy as they say he is. Handsome but hairy. A real
sasquatch."
Katie laughed out loud. It surprised her. It had been
a long time since she'd heard herself laugh. Only
Lucy, her oldest friend, could really make her laugh
like that these days. Now that Katie was engaged to
the divine and erudite banker, Oliver Hurst- Wyatt,
she found she rarely laughed out loud anymore. She
never went anywhere that it was appropriate.

Certainly, Oliver didn't appreciate emotional outbursts of any kind.

Yet, he was worth it. A real catch. Again, Katie congratulated herself on being perfectly positioned in life, a winner. Yes, Katherine Hurst -Wyatt did have a lovely sound to it. She found herself fondling her engagement ring. It was a beauty and had once belonged to his grandmother.

"You'd hate Daniel's look. I know you like them shorn and shaved, is that look still called metrosexual? Am I allowed to say metrosexual?" Lucy rummaged around in one of her bags, took out a lip balm and proceeded to emulsify her lips. Katie gazed on. She would never dream of applying makeup or preening herself in public. What would people think?

It was true, Oliver was extremely well groomed, rather more so than Katie in many ways. He was often late for dates because of his preparations but he was well worth the wait. He was beautiful to look at- all Swedish chiselled bones and dark blonde hair. And he was, Katie searched for the word, *precise*. Even on the night he proposed, Christmas Eve, he'd brought a napkin from the restaurant and laid it out on the floor, so that he could kneel on it without damaging his Armani suit. Of course Katie, emotionally bright as a whip, knew as soon as she saw the napkin that something was up. She had waited patiently and acted surprised when the moment finally came. No, Oliver wasn't given over to rash shows of emotion.

In fairness, Lucy had already suggested that this might be "the night" and that Katie should have her nails done and wear her best Roksanda dress- that was girl-code in action right there. She trusted Lucy. "Are you still going to that will reading tomorrow? Your aunt's?" Lucy said, fiddling inside her bag and emerging with a tissue.

"Yes. Goodness knows what that's all about. I don't really have time for any of it but I must admit, I am intrigued."

Katie's Aunt Liza had died unexpectedly a few weeks earlier. Katie felt a pang of regret at the fact that she hadn't taken the time to get to know her better while she was alive but reassured herself with the fact that she had a very busy career in the city. She couldn't do everything. And, besides, they'd never been close. Not really. There had actually been no contact since her own mother had cut Aunt Liza out of her life twenty-five years previously. Her own sister! And Katie's mother had refused to explain why. Just said that Liza had become: "a mean old cow, and prudish with it."

Aunt Liza had run a small holding in Devon whereas Katie's mother, Veronica, "Ronnie" had moved to London and tried to hold down a variety of short term, low paid jobs all the while doing her best to secure a rich boyfriend. The fact that she was considered by many to be extremely beautiful tended to work for her in this regard.

"Is your mother still with that pro tennis coach in Tenerife?" Lucy enquired.

"Yep, and the longer she stays out there the better for all of us," Katie said knowingly. "Makes my life that much less complicated."

Katie had always been more of a grown up than her mother.

"Is that where you grew up then?" Lucy asked. "Devon?"

"We didn't live there very long."

Katie had lived at Butterfly Farm for a short time. One of mother's boyfriends, who had turned out not to be as wealthy, or as nice, as he had pretended, refused to leave their dingy maisonette in Walthamstow and, in an emergency flit, they had been taken in by Aunt Liza.

Butterfly Farm sounded beautiful but was in fact a rundown animal sanctuary, which her mother quickly came to despise. Katie however had loved it. She still smiled at the thought of all the fun she'd had exploring the nearby fields. Living on the farm for those short weeks had been freeing; memories that were youthful and joyous. She had learnt how to feed lambs, collect eggs and make dens with the Baker boys from the next farm along. What had been their names, again?

Ah, yes, Henry, and of course her first crush, James

Baker.

Yes, James Baker, a year older and her first real sweetheart. They had built a den and hung out reading comics and talking about what they would do when they were older. She clearly remembered James saying that when he was rich he'd eat fish and chips from the mobile van every day of the week. How funny. It had been an innocent time when she would stay out all day, only returning to the farm once it got dark. James would often walk her to the gate on Hackhurst Lane. The one which separated their two farms.

He'd nearly kissed her once, leaned in so close that she felt his breath on her face. Sitting on the train, her legs went tingly just at the thought of it.

"Katie?"

"Yes, yes," Katie was roused from the memory. "It's all very odd, she's put in her letter of wishes that she wants a public reading of the will. And she specifically asked for me to be there. Goodness knows why or even who else is going to be there."

Perhaps Farmer Baker with James and Henry in tow?

"Your mum?"

"You're joking – she didn't even come back for Liza's funeral – she's not interested. She didn't even tell me she was dead. That was down to Wilsons solicitors getting in touch, otherwise I wouldn't have known."

"Is Ollie going with you?

"I've asked but he's not got back to me. Good

thinking though, Batman," Katie removed her phone from her Cartier tote bag and tapped his number, "Ollie?"

An overly loud voice boomed – "Just a minute I'll take it outside." Music was playing in the distance. Katie pouted, waiting.

Lucy widened her eyes and looked away across the carriage in a feigned attempt to give her some privacy.

"Ollie, where are you? "

"Got to pull an all-nighter. The whole team is on standby for the markets opening. Grabbing a drink then back to it."

Katie couldn't hide her disappointment. She wouldn't see him now and that meant she'd be on her own again tonight. This was happening more and more nowadays. For a happily engaged girl she was starting to feel like a lonely singleton.

"Ollie, I was wondering if you'd thought about coming to my aunt's will reading tomorrow. I know you're super busy but.."

Suddenly a woman's voice in the background "Oliver, Oliver, come on darling." A clink of glasses and a long pause. Then a loud outburst of background laughter.

"Sorry Katie, I've got to go. We're… er, well." He was desperately looking for a believable narrative and she knew from his stuttering phrasing that he was trying to hide something. "We're celebrating the Cookson deal going through today, that's all."

13

"Oliver, come on! Marco has ordered another three bottles of Krug!" the giggling woman drew closer to the phone.

"Shush!" he responded.

"Is that Waitey Katie?" the drunken woman whispered. And then loudly, impatiently, "Oh just tell her the truth, Oliver. Tell her about *us.* "

There was the sound of the handset being momentarily being covered – Oliver was clearly trying to placate the woman. "Look, just go back inside."

Katie's mind raced. She took a deep breath.

"Oliver, who is that?"

A wave of shock started to run through her.

"What is she talking about?" Katie turned to Lucy who, having heard the exchange grimaced and gave Katie a pitying look.

He gave a long, exasperated sigh.

"Katie, we need to talk. I need to tell you… "an awkward silence. "Look, we really need to talk about this, but…"

There was a long pause. Katie began to shake, a mixture of disbelief and shock.

She pressed the 'End' button and sat silently looking at the screen saver. It was a selfie she'd taken of her and Oliver smiling in Regents Park.

The whole carriage was suddenly silent. Everything moving in slow motion. Her mind raced to piece together all his unusual behaviours over the past month. The little lies that he'd let slip, the late nights

14

and vague excuses. It was all making sense now.

He was seeing someone else.

The realisation hit her like a pain in the chest and for the first time since childhood she put her head down and wept.

She was in total shock.

In that moment Katie knew, really knew, despite all of her subconscious denials of his behaviours, that the dream of being married to Oliver was just that: a ridiculous dream.

Another relationship ending in failure.

At thirty-six she would soon be too old to even think about having a family.

Was she destined to always be alone?

On seeing her, Lucy's eyes also brimmed with tears and she hugged Katie as hard as she could, bracing her as the sobs began to spill out.

Chapter two

The door of the large Georgian building which housed Wilson's solicitors stood open and Katie stepped through into the marbled reception area. It was a beautiful building and she found herself wondering, not for the first time, how Liza had managed to afford this level of service.

"Katherine?"

An older man with grey hair moved towards her, hand outstretched.

"Yes, that's right," she said taking his hand.

"Welcome to Wilsons. I'm Michael Dasher, in charge of administering your aunt's estate. Thank you for coming and can I begin by saying I'm so sorry for your loss."

He tipped his head downwards in a gesture of respect.

"Oh, thank you," she said, before leaning forward and whispering. "But I must admit I didn't really know her all that well."

"Really?" he appeared genuinely surprised, "Well, oh well. Well that is a strange set of circumstances then. She talked about you an awful lot."

To hide his confusion, he turned to indicate a side room where refreshments had been laid out. "Tea? Coffee?"

"No thank you. What is? What is strange?"

He looked like he was about to tell her but then quickly put his finger to his lips. "No, no, time for all that later. Please, would you like to come up? Some of the others are already here."

And to think, she almost hadn't come. After a dreadful night's sleep, being woken by drunken voice notes from Oliver, she had told work she would get into the office by the afternoon. They owed her that much anyhow- she had weeks of holiday owing. She was determined that she would have no more contact with Ollie until she felt a little more rested. And ticking this will reading off her list would help her to clear her head.

Mr. Dasher led her, with faltering steps, up a curving balustraded staircase. Upon reaching the landing, they proceeded along into a huge end room with wide windows running along the entire back wall. A large, antique-looking desk faced a number of plush, red velvet seats. Katie was invited to slide into a row. She placed her bag on the floor and took a deep breath to settle her nerves. She didn't know why she was nervous, only that she was.

On her right were a number of "tweeded" men. They looked like proper farming types. One caught her eye. He tipped his flat cap at her in what she took to be a sign of condolence. She nodded in return. There were various couples, she assumed, from the village. They sat in a tidy silence, hushed by the seriousness of the surroundings

On her left was an older woman with a mound of grey unkempt hair who was clearly upset. She was continually dabbing her eyes with strips of toilet tissue she took from a large tapestry-style bag. There were knitting needles poking out the top.

A young girl, possibly around sixteen years old but very childlike - grasped the old woman's arm. Her head moved erratically, eyes darting left and right. She turned to Katie at that moment smiled and then mouthed, "Hello" in an exaggerated fashion. Katie smiled back. The girl had a lovely, wild energy about her.

It seemed that everyone knew who she was, while, for her part, Katie recognised no one.

"Thank you all for coming," Mr Dasher took centre stage behind the desk. "Elizabeth would be very pleased that so many people have decided to make the effort." He opened a large manila folder before scanning the room. "Well, I think we're almost all here. Shall we begin?"

He sat up regally, clearly enjoying the pomp and ceremony.

"Elizabeth Reynolds, Liza to her friends was a wonderful woman…"

Katie, eased herself back into her seat. This might take some time.

There was a crash from behind them, followed by the sound of someone bundling through the rear doors.

"Sorry, we're late."

A deep booming voice.

Mr. Dasher indicated for whoever it was to take a seat and Katie, irritated with the manner of their entrance, turned to see who it might be. This clumsy idiot.

And there he was …. James, James Baker.

At 6-foot six, a mighty bear of a man. Despite his size, his face was still familiar, even though the dark growth of his beard.

The last time she had seen him he was chasing some boys who had wrecked their den. A den which they'd played in happily for weeks, telling ghost stories while trying to work out how to start a fire. She hadn't known that that would be their last time together. She'd never had a chance to say goodbye.

As she was thinking this, his brother Henry appeared. The two of them crouched down, sloping into the seats on the row in front. Henry turned and smiled at Katie. He nudged James to try and get his attention, bobbing his head in Katie's direction.

And then James turned. And that was when he saw her, saw her properly. He gave her a polite, almost sheepish smile. She suddenly felt very hot and completely thrown. For a moment her head was swimming and she had to force herself to try and focus on what Mr Dasher was saying at the front of the room.

Only she couldn't quite manage it.

Mr Dasher's voice droned on, drowned out by the sound of the blood pumping through her ears. Something about Liza saving animals and receiving an MBE. Gifts she'd previously bestowed on certain individuals.

Katie was shocked to realise that she knew virtually nothing about this woman. She just couldn't make sense of it. Why hadn't she known more about her?

"And she wanted you to know that you all played a very special part in her life. "

Katie was still distracted and glanced over in James's direction. She suddenly felt very self-aware, like a young girl. He looked back at her and held her gaze. She felt her cheeks begin to warm as something rose up in her.

" Now to the larger assets. Jean…"

The older woman straightened her posture to listen. Dasher continued to read, "I would like to thank you for all of your tireless help with the farm by asking you to carry on helping there for as long as you can or want to. Although, obviously, that will depend on whether the new owners would like you to. You have lived rent free in my Tumbledown Cottage along the lane for many years. "

Jean nodded solemnly and held her breath.

"You may of course continue to stay there, on the same rent-free basis, for as long as you choose to." Jean slumped forward with relief. "In any event, I have made arrangements that your beloved granddaughter Maisie will inherit that cottage on your death. "

"Ooh that's me, that's me! "the younger girl blurted out, laughing, thrilled with the mention of her name. Jean wept openly. Clearly, Liza had done something very kind and generous.

A cottage? Liza had owned a cottage? Katie had thought that the farm was tied and Liza had as little money and property as her mother. How wrong had she been?

But what was Katie doing there? What was she expecting? Family trinkets? Photographs?

"For you all - I have arranged for Jim at "The Red Lion" to receive a thousand pounds in order to organise a night of drinks, dancing and celebration where all of you, my wonderful neighbours can celebrate, for once, without me."

There was much hilarity from the gentlemen on Katie's right.

"Good Ol 'Liza," one old voice boomed.

"That's great Jim!" said one old man dressed in tweed

to the man beside him.

"Ay, I'll give her a great send off." Jim was a squat, pink faced man who raised a hanky to his eye.

Mr Dasher steadied himself by placing both palms flat on the desk, ready for his grand finale.

"And finally, the farm."

A hush descended.

"I have only loved two things in my life wholly and goodly. Katherine, you were the daughter I never had." Katie became completely still and alert. "I am so proud of how you have conducted yourself your whole life, in sometimes very challenging circumstances. I have followed your education and career closely."

Mr Dasher paused for dramatic effect then looked directly at her. It took Katie a beat to realise where he was going with this.

"I leave you my other love: Butterfly Farm, the whole lovely ramshackle lot of it to do with as you see fit." There was a sharp intake of breath from around the room – it was clearly a huge bequest. Mr Dasher nodded his approval.

" You will own all two hundred and eighty acres, farmhouse, outbuildings and assets therein.

The only stipulation being, that you must not sell it within one calendar year of the date of this reading. I hope whatever you do makes you as truly happy as I have been."

All eyes turned to Katie and for a moment she

thought she might faint. Because of the Oliver debacle the night before she hadn't really eaten or slept. Her eyes started to lose focus and she felt herself start to slump.

Oh, she was fainting.

Suddenly a huge arm engulfed her and she was gently pulled back into her seat. It was James. He had his arm around her and was gently whispering, "You're ok, steady now." His dark eyes looked straight into hers, willing her to recover. Someone forced a bottle of water into her hand. Just as suddenly as he had saved her, James was gone and instead kindly Mr. Dasher was beaming down at her.

Chapter three

"So what happened then?" Lucy slowly stirred her coffee watching Katie with growing awe. The pair sat at a cute café table along Dulwich High Street completely in their own bubble, cut off from the busy world outside.

"To be honest, Lucy, it was all a bit of a blur. You know when you go to the doctor and they tell you something important but then you can't remember it because you're too over stimulated? Well, it was like that. Of course, on top of what happened with Ollie, it just all feels like some kind of bad dream."

"Well, that James sounds like a proper dream boat."

"Lucy! How old are you? Nobody uses the word *dreamboat* anymore - that went out with old black and white movies."

"Nothing wrong with a real man who makes a

woman feel… womanly"

"I don't need a man to make me feel womanly," Katie said firmly signalling the end of that conversation by determinedly drinking her coffee. Lucy looked hurt.

Katie softened. "Seriously though Lucy," looking forlornly at the huge set of keys that dominated the middle of the café table. "What am I going to do? I haven't got time to even think about this- I can't keep on top of my own laundry let alone…" Her voice trailed off and she pushed one of the old, rusted keys around the central ring. Then she looked at the residue which had come off on her fingers with a kind of disgust. "What does this even open?"

"Well, it seems to me you have two options" Lucy straightened, taking her role of advisor very seriously. "One, leave London and throw yourself into Ye Olde Devon ways." Katie gave an exasperated sigh at that. "Or two, and much easier, pay a farm manager for a year, then sell it and enjoy spending the money." Katie flared her nostrils in thought. "Actually, it might not even be a year."

"I thought you said…"

"Hmm, I know that's what Liza wanted. Trouble is, apparently, the National Highways Agency are reconnoitring in the South Devon area. They're considering a buyout of parts of the countryside to extend the road network through Devon and into Cornwall."

"A compulsory purchase order?

"Exactly."

Lucy's eyes narrowed and she chimed, "Well, even better. That would mean big money, no guilt, and a sharp exit!"

Lucy held her coffee cup up in a mock toast.

"Yes, you're right," reflected Katie." And dismissed an intrusive thought about "Lovely Liza" as the two cups clinked together.

Chapter four

By the time Katie returned to the office, it was after three pm but she had correspondence to catch up on and liked to keep on top of her billable hours. Yes, she'd work late in an effort to grab back some control. It wasn't as if she had anyone waiting for her at home or eager to take her out to dinner.

She sat at her desk, willing herself to focus on the words on the screen. Suddenly James Baker's face flashed in front of her. She was losing it, clearly losing it. Bizarrely Ollie wasn't featuring in her thoughts anymore, almost as if she had compartmentalised him away. Cut him off for her own survival. She would also have to deal with all the apology texts he kept sending at some point.

She settled down to a couple of hours of quality work, focussed and alert. She was good at her job and enjoyed the intellectual stimulation of contentious law. She liked a fight and a cause to get behind.

"Katie!" Simon Martindale bundled into her office, his pink shirt stretched taut across his ever-widening stomach, his tie askew.

"Katie, glad you're still here. How did the reading go?" He didn't wait for a reply. "Anyhoo," he had clearly been drinking. "A few of us are next door having a little celebration. Feel free to pop in. There's someone I'd like you to meet."

And with that he grabbed a bottle of water from her desk before rebounding off the doorframe on his way out, back to his office.

Oh no, Katie thought, she didn't have the armour in place to deal with Simon Martindale's antics right now. She'd show her face and leave with excuses, whatever the occasion. Another new girlfriend, perhaps?

She slipped her Manolo's back on, wrestled her jacket off the chair, retrieved her bag and readied herself.

There were numerous people in the conference room, drinking freely from the bottles of champagne which ranged over the table. A number of senior team members were chatting animatedly with one another. Peter Smith, one of the more decent senior associates acknowledged Katie's arrival. The beautiful and up thrusting Sophie La Cruz was holding court for some reason. "Yes, I can speak five languages fluently," was how she had once introduced herself to

Katie. How had Katie missed this invite? Yes, she had been distracted by Oliver and the will but it was not like her to miss a networking event on this scale. What the hell was going on?

She found a corner to secrete herself and Martindale's PA, a sweet woman called Gemma, handed Katie a glass. "Heard you had a big day."

"And you don't know the half of it."

"Really? Are you okay? "

"I will be, just had my complete world turned upside down in the space of twenty-four hours."

"Actually then Katie, perhaps I should tell you that.."

"Gem, Gemma dear girl," Simon's voice crescendoed around the room. "More champagne if you wouldn't mind."

Gemma pulled a strained face to Katie who nodded in solidarity as Gemma turned back to her duties.

"So, ladies and gentlemen just a little welcome party for Sophie, the lovely Sophie. Please raise a glass." Sophie was at the top of the table in a figure-hugging black dress. She moved in an exaggerated swaying motion with sweet smiles as if all too eager to please. The men understandably couldn't keep their eyes off her, she looked fabulous. "Welcome Sophie."

What was he on about? She'd been in the firm for eighteen months at least.

"Welcome to being a full partner at Martindale's. And yes, everyone, finally, we have a girlie on the board." And with that the room held their glasses high while the men gave a good-natured cheer.

Katie involuntarily started to raise her glass as well, only stopping when the full implication of what was happening finally hit home.

She'd been side lined.

Gemma reached over and began filling Katie's glass, grimacing in a show of sympathy.

"To Sophie!" they all chimed. Only Katie was silent.

Chapter five

The drive down to Devon seemed to take forever. *They really do need better road links down here*, Katie mused as she wound her way South. She had gone on the run for her own survival. She needed time to focus on her needs.

She had spent the night trying to remember what she had originally wanted for herself and how this whole sorry mess had started. Somehow she had got lost in the day-to-day minutia of being an adult and had simply lost sight of herself. The past days had been unreal.

She pulled into a service station to check her phone messages before deciding that she may as well get herself a coffee and a cheese sandwich. If in doubt eat cheese. She wandered around the small concessions which only seemed to sell bizarre items like reading glasses and neck rests. She was tired, really tired.

Back in the car, she rang the office. How could she have been so wrong about a possible promotion? She had been absolutely blindsided by Sophie la Cruz's mercurial rise through the ranks. It was as if she couldn't trust her own judgement anymore.

"Hi Gemma, it's me again, Katie."

"Hi Katie- I've put your holidays on the system now and let your team know, like you asked me to. You ok?"

"I will be." Katie slipped her partly eaten sandwich back onto its wrapper and placed it on the seat next to her. She took a deep breath, "Keep it to yourself but I'm heading down to Devon for a few days. I want to have a look around before I decide what to do."

"Oh, really. I thought you lawyers all went to exotic islands for your holidays. Well, hurry back, I don't think I can keep going without another woman in the office. Simon has been worse than ever after all that champagne he drank last night."

"Sorry, Gem. I'll keep up with my clients whilst I'm down here through emails though I'm not sure about my wireless connections down here in the sticks. Can you put some delaying tactics in place and give me some space?"

"Of course! Let me know if there's anything else I can do. And Katie…"

"Yes?"

"Try and enjoy yourself."

*

The roads got narrower and narrower. At some points Katie wasn't sure that her Audi would even get through. A couple of times weird machinery, like combine harvesters dominated whole sections of the road. She was determined to find the house and then have a look for the nearest bed and breakfast.

It took an age to drive the last few miles and as Katie passed the sign for Dunsford Village she felt a wave of exhaustion wash over her. She parked along the high street, near a pub called The White Horse. The directions to The Reynolds Farm, which had been renamed Butterfly Farm in the fifties, was confusing. It seemed to be weirdly off an unadopted road called Hackhurst Lane. What did unadopted even mean? If she hadn't had second thoughts about coming down here previously, she did now. Katie needed her sleep, she was a grouch when she didn't get enough and everything got out of wonk. The odd thing was that closer she got to the farm the further away it seemed. There was nobody even around to ask. She turned off her engine, stretched her neck backwards and felt very sorry for herself. Lucy had said she'd have been happy to go with her if she could wait until the weekend but Katie knew she had to get away. People

33

tended to underestimate Katie. They seemed to assume that she'd always led a very privileged life when, in reality, she'd had to work for everything she'd ever achieved. It gave her an inner resilience which she could call on when times got tough.

"'Ello?" A man was tapping at her window. She must have fallen asleep. Katie jumped up as if she had been caught out.

"Oh hello," she wound her window down.

"You okay, lady?"

Katie sat up straight in her seat. "Yes, just a very long drive."

"Where you heading?"

Katie thought that this was quite an intrusive question. That wouldn't happen in East Dulwich.

"Butterfly Farm." And then with more emphasis, "I'm the new owner."

The man nodded, "Liza's niece?"

Of course he knew Liza, how stupid of her. "Yes, that's right."

He nodded, "I seen you at that lawyer's place. You fainted."

"Nearly," she replied, suddenly embarrassed.

"Yes, well, good luck to you, girl."

And with that he went to move off.

"Excuse me?" she called out to stop him. He turned. "Can you tell me where it is?"

"The farm? You mean, you don't know?"

Obviously, she didn't know. What was he thinking?

"No. The sat nav keeps sending me to here."

He paused. "She was a great woman, you know."

"So I believe."

"Go up Smithfield's Road then sharp right down Hackhurst Lane. The farm is on the right. I think weeds have grown over all the signs."

"Thank you," she said. "Sorry, and you are Mr…"

"Riley, Jim Riley. I run the White Horse."

"Thank you, I…" but he'd already turned and left.

*

It was getting towards sunset as Katie pulled down Hackhurst Lane on her final approach to Butterfly Farm. She had no idea which of the numerous keys that Mr. Dasher had handed over would get her into the farm or the house. The sun was a mottled pink under a duvet of reflective clouds and Katie was relieved to be nearly at her destination.

Suddenly, a man emerged from a field over on her left. Without looking, he walked straight out into the road, moving away from her. She braked sharply and chided herself for losing concentration so late in the journey.

Next thing, the road was completely blocked as a herd of cows, udders swaying beneath their bellies, brushed past her car, totally fixed on following the man down the lane. There had to be thirty of them, no doubt heading off to the milking shed.

As the final stragglers wandered out, a farm hand appeared, closing the gate as he hastened to catch up with the group. He turned to absently thank her for waiting, raised his hand then stopped dead.

It was him.

James Baker.

He approached the car and stood next to her window. She smiled. He didn't. He indicated that perhaps she should wind down the window.

"Oh, yes, sorry," she said. The electric window slowly wound down.

"Hello Katie."

"Hello."

He leaned in closer, looking a little baffled. "Only, I didn't think I was ever going to see you again."

 A pause.

Then he said, "Let alone down here."

"Yes, no. What I mean is …" she was struggling to rationalise her thoughts. "I've come to have a look at the place. "

And, as an afterthought, she softened, "I think it's what Liza would have wanted."

Goodness that sounded so insincere.

"You're right," he nodded. "She would."

 What else was there to say? The silence was palpable and awkward.

 "Anyhow," he broke in. "Gotta get on. These cows won't milk themselves."

"I know they need it every day don't they!" she

blurted out, desperate to find some common ground. "Actually twice a day."

She pulled a face to show her incompetence and laughed at herself. He, for his part, kept a straight face. Then he pushed himself up from the window and began to back away.

"I hope you get the farm sorted out as quickly as possible," he said, looking her straight in the eye. "It's affected everybody, being left in that state."

There was a moment of stillness under the darkening sky. Those same deep eyes.

And the next moment he was gone, jogging along the lane to catch up with the stragglers. He didn't look back.

Chapter six

By the time Katie pulled up in front of the farmhouse the light was going but she could still make out a lot of detail from the light of the moon. The grey farm outhouses ran all the way down the right-hand side with a series of large, metal sheds extending even further back. Already the place seemed bigger than she remembered.

The farm gate had been open wide, thankfully, and the faded wooden sign saying, "Butterfly Farm-Reynolds Est. 1847," had reassured her that this was the place.

She removed her small Gucci case from the boot and turned the on the torch on her phone. Luckily, as she stumbled along the uneven, dirty path which lead towards the farmhouse, a security light flashed on, scaring her momentarily. But then, when she'd gotten over the shock, she found that at least now she could see well enough to find a door key which might actually fit.

Once she got to the front door, she started methodically trying each key, one after the other. But as darkness started to close in all around her, she thought she could hear something from over in the yard. Animal sounds. Various scrapings and whinnying. Of course, the animals, they were still being housed here. But that was the first time she'd actually thought about it. About them. The animals and practicalities of caring for them. If nothing else, the smell should have alerted her.

"The stink of the countryside!" her mother's voice echoed round her head. Was it too late to find a hotel room?

Then came a satisfying click as one of the keys engaged with the lock, turning easily. As she tried to push the door open, a thick pile of accumulated letters prevented her and she was forced to move the door back and forth in order to create a big enough gap for her to squeeze through.

Once inside, she stooped to pick up a handful of mail, dropping them on a dusty console table. She noticed that a lot of the letters were red banded with some having Final Notice printed across the front. Finding a switch, she gave a little prayer that somehow the electricity might still be connected. And then, when she flicked the switch, gave a little squeal as the light came on. The place was old. Old fashioned and musty. For a moment she was anxious, finding herself totally alone in an old unwelcoming house. But then, she steeled herself and, placing her foot against the back of the door, eased it shut. Now all she had to do was venture inside.

She headed for the kitchen and on turning on the light, found a large room dominated by the huge pine table at its centre. There was an old sofa and a fire on one side of the room and units, sink and what she thought must be some kind of Aga under one of the big rickety windows. She suddenly felt very exposed and hurried to close the curtains. She was simply too exhausted to think about heading out again but decided she wouldn't be venturing upstairs tonight. Her imagination would only punish her if she did. The sofa would have to do.

"Well, Liza, here I am," she said out loud.

After boiling a kettle and finding some dusty tea bags, she sat at the table and poured herself a hot drink. She was completely alone in the middle of nowhere. And who actually cared? She looked down at her black tea. There was no milk in the fridge but at least it had been cleaned and turned off so nothing nasty had been able to grow. Tomorrow she would have be a real adult and do things. Stock up with supplies, get in some food.

Milk.

James.

She warmed as she thought of their encounter on the roadside but continued to be puzzled about his lack of care towards her. Men usually liked getting to know her. She'd had plenty of boyfriends and she often found herself dismissing unwanted advances. But James?

Well, he was another case altogether. Just not interested.

The phone buzzed to life, catching her off guard.

"Lucy!"

"How are you my intrepid little adventurer? Are you there yet?"

"I am, and I'm sitting with a cup of tea."

"Oh good. Is it how you remember it?

"Yes, and no. I thought it was smaller than this – the house itself is massive and then there's all the farm buildings, all the land. Goodness knows how big the place is."

"So, you're richer than you thought. I always knew one day I'd have a rich friend. "

"Don't get carried away, from what I can see, there's a pile of red notices from all the utility companies. God knows what's going on there."

"Oh well, I'm sure you'll get all that sorted, Katie, you are the most organised and resourceful woman I know." There was a subtle softening of her tone. "I actually think Liza has been very generous here. Not just in leaving you the house, but in, well, thinking of you as an actual person. Thinking about what might

41

make *you* happy."

"I am not staying!" Katie said in mock defiance and laughed.

"I know, I know it's not the life for you but how fun to see what it would be like to be someone else for a little while. To try something different for a couple of weeks and see, just see. You need some time to recharge your batteries, Katie."

"Yes, you might be right there," Katie absently looked down and noticed the state of her shoes. "Lucy, I've got muck all over my Moncler shoes, animal muck!"

Lucy laughed uproariously. "I'll be down soon. You can moan about it all then."

"What are you up to then?"

"I've got a wellbeing weekend booked with some people from work: yoga, meditation, you know the sort of thing. Unfortunately, all alcohol free."

"And is the delectable Daniel Beardsley going to be there? How's that going, by the way?"

"As a matter of fact he is, and," she lowered her voice to a whisper. "It's all going VERY well."

"Lucy, why are you whispering?"

"Oh, you know I jinx everything! I don't want the Universe to spite me for bragging. As it is, the office all call me Mrs Speak Too Soon."

"Lucy, have you heard anything about Ollie? I was going to speak to him but it's been too stressful. I just didn't have the capacity."

"He's stopped leaving messages now, so at least he's recognised that I need some time to think. I'm still not sure what - if anything - has actually happened. And I wonder if it's something we can come back from. Perhaps work on."

There was a silence.

"Lucy?"

A sigh. "Let's talk about it tomorrow. You sound really tired."

"You're right, tomorrow."

Chapter seven

It was dawn. The sun streamed through the thin curtains and Katie could hear a motor running. A tractor? She sat up on the sofa, pushing aside the blanket she had wrapped herself in and undid her coat. She had slept quite well considering she was somewhere completely different and not sleeping in a proper bed.

She stretched upwards, stood up and headed to the window. Someone was moving around the yard outside and off to the left she could see a quad bike heading off down a side lane.

What should she do now? What was the protocol of introducing yourself as the new owner?

She headed to the downstairs loo and, using the little cracked sink, managed to splash her face with cold water. There was a hand towel hanging up that said

Washed Up! on it in thin, silvery letters and she gently patted her face with it. She hadn't even thought to bring a towel. She really should have stayed at a hotel last night. But then again, she was here now.

Finding a pair of wellingtons which pretty much fitted, Katie headed out into the yard. In wellington boots, she realised that she moved like a yeti.

"Hello!" she called out to the figure pushing a wheelbarrow across the yard. "Hello?"

The figure turned towards her, looking startled. It was the woman who'd been at the will reading. Jean. She dropped the wheelbarrow to the ground.

"Goodness," Jean said. "Good morning. Katie, isn't it? I wondered if that was your car out front- very nice. Don't often see posh cars down this way. All big muddy things down here. "

"Yes, that is mine, thank you" Katie moved towards her. "How are you, Jean?"

Jean was thrilled to be remembered, "Yes, very well, thank you. Of course it's not the same without Liza. We loved Liza."

Katie went over to her and touched her arm. Jean dropped her head..

"I'm sure she knew that," Katie said.

"She did. She really did."

Katie decided to move the conversation to a more upbeat subject. "So, who's that heading up the lane and where are you going with all of this, er, wheat?"

"Straw."

"Straw. Straw, of course."

"Well, that's Maisie going up to the chicken sheds, she likes driving that bike. Liza put her in charge of getting the eggs. She collects 'em, sizes 'em, then sells them down the village. We make a lot of money from them eggs."

"Really?" Katie suddenly remembered the pile of bills she'd seen the previous night. "Like, how much money?"

"Oh, she can make £25 per week, easy."

"Oh! Right."

Jean could hear the disappointment in her voice. "But we do get other money coming in, too."

"Let's talk about this later, Jean."

"Yes, let me just feed the pigs and I'll make you some eggs for breakfast. "

"That would be really lovely- I'm starving."

Jean hoisted up her wheelbarrow again, pleased to have said the right thing and made her way over to the first barn. As she pulled open the large wooden doors, the noise from the animals was genuinely disconcerting.

"Morning my little darlings!" Jean shouted and turned to wave at Katie as she headed in.

Katie smiled, but inside she knew that she was completely out of her depth.

*

Jean was deftly frying up eggs in a big black pan. They were the yellowest yolks that Katie had ever

seen and the smell of frying food was irresistible.
Katie hadn't realised how hungry she was.

Maisie sat at the farmhouse table next to Katie,
stroking the very expensive overnight bag that Katie
had brought with her.

"Is this a makeup bag?" Maisie asked. "Is this *your*
makeup? "

She took out a jar of Crème de Mer skin cream and
opened the lid, removing a lump of white cream with
her finger

"Yes, yes, all my girl stuff," Katie replied quickly,
deftly taking the jar back from her before Maisie used
the lot. That was one month's egg profits right there!

"Maisie, tell me what you do on the farm?" she asked,
sliding her over-night bag under the table.

"I like the animals," Maisie said, rubbing the cream
into her neck and face. Only, she hadn't taken the
time to wash and so, the mud which had been on her
chin, was now being spread all over her face.

"Oh, Maisie," Jean exclaimed upon seeing her. "Look
at the state of you! Go and wash your face. Now!"

With a roll of her eyes, Maisie got up and headed to
the bathroom.

"She loved being in London," Jean said. "She
couldn't believe all those women wearing high heels!"

"I know how she feels," laughed Katie." I have a
sort-of love, hate relationship with them myself."

Jean smiled, putting a plate down in front of Katie.
As well as tomatoes and mushrooms, there were two

47

fried eggs. How had she rustled all this up so quickly? Katie couldn't remember the last time someone had cooked for her outside of a catered dinner party.

She scooped up some mushrooms with her fork and started to chew. They tasted delicious.

"Jean, you're a life saver."

When Maisie returned, the three of them sat around chatting while Jean filled their mugs with coffee.

Then, she told Katie about Liza and her struggle to keep the farm over the last few years and how Jean thought that Liza had actually died of stress, rather than the breast cancer that had been written on her death certificate.

"She liked to laugh," Jean said. "She liked to drink, she liked to dance and she liked to laugh."

"I wish I'd known her better."

"Oh, she talked about you," cried Maisie. "She talked about you all the time!"

Jean touched Maisie's arm to get her to stop.

"There's plenty of time for all that later, my darling."

"Is she staying, nan? Are you staying Katie?

Katie felt suddenly torn. No, she was going to have to tell the truth.

"To be honest Maisie, no. I'm not."

Masie's head dropped.

Katie turned to Jean. "I have a life in London, a career, a boyfriend."

She realised that she was trying to reason with them. Trying to make sense of it all.

"Of course," Jean nodded sadly. "We didn't really expect you to stay."

She stood up and slowly began to collect the plates.

"I did," chimed in Maisie, "It's a lovely place to live."

Katie felt something loosen inside her. She reached over and stroked Maisie's cheek.

"That feels smoother already."

*

Katie couldn't believe how charming the village of Dunsford was. It was wonderfully picturesque and had the added advantage that, at exactly twelve midday, the churches in the surrounding villages rang their bells creating a magical effect.

She managed to get some basic provisions from the village shop. It was a charming little place that smelt of bread and fresh fruit with everything displayed in various wooden boxes. The woman who worked there was smiley and was curious to know who Katie was without asking her directly. Katie put her out of her misery by confirming that she had come down to sell Butterfly Farm.

"Thought so," said the woman. "I'm Jackie. I work here part time and then over at the nursery in Holcot." Katie nodded. "You got any children?"

"No," Katie shook her head thoughtfully. She'd never been asked that question quite so directly before. "No babies, I'm afraid."

"Shame."

Why did that hurt Katie? But it did hurt.

Loaded with milk, bread and chocolate topped with a load of toilet rolls, she made her way back to the car.

"Good morning Missy Katie," it was the man who'd given her directions the previous night. "You found your way to the farm alright then?"

"Oh yes, thank you so much. I was at my wits end trying to find it," she was having difficulty balancing all her shopping.

"It is off the beaten track, I'll give you that." The man reached out to help her with the toilet rolls which were in danger of over-balancing. "Let me help you back to your car with these."

"Thank you. I wasn't planning to stay the night there but it was too late to go to a hotel by the time I realised."

"So you are planning on staying then?"

"For a short while at least. I need to get a farm manager in to sort it all out. So I thought that actually being here would be a good start."

Jim nodded sagely.

"Do you know anyone I might approach locally? "

"I'll have a think about it," he paused. "Would it be worth your while though? We all know now that the Highways agency are looking at buying the land. Wouldn't it be best to just run the farm down until the compulsory purchase order comes through?"

"Has that all been decided then?"

"That's what people round here have been saying."

"Running it down? What do you mean by running it down?" Katie asked.

"Well, get rid of the animals at the very least."

"Yes," Katie mused. "The animals."

When she got back, she really should go round the whole farm and see how many animals there actually were. If she did intend to sell up, the very least she'd have to do would be to ensure that all the animals had new homes.

Katie's phone rang out.

"Sorry, thank you for your help, if you wouldn't mind asking around for a manager I'd be grateful. I'm not a natural farmer myself." She laughed aloud at this as it was such an obvious observation. He nodded but then seemed a little disappointed in her. She realised that for some reason she'd misjudged her response. She held up her phone. "I have to take this."

Jim gave Katie a thumbs up signal and then closed the boot on her shopping.

"Lucy, just a min."

She manoeuvred herself into the driving seat and shut the door.

"Juggling loo roll here. Go ahead, how are you?"

"Good, I've just arrived at the Sudbury House place for my wellbeing thing. And,"

she paused for comic effect. "Manged to smuggle in a bottle of prosecco."

"Naughty girl, who are you planning on sharing that with?"

"Mr. Sasquatch."

Katie laughed. "Lucy, you are incorrigible."

"I know. How's it going with you?"

"Apart from sleeping in a cold, scary house and being completely out of my depth, everything's fine! Lucy, really what am I doing?" She watched Jim walk back along the High Street. She had no idea how to handle any of this.

"Your best, Katie. You're doing your best."

Good old Lucy – number one cheer leader.

"Katie, I've got some news about Ollie. "There was a pause. "Do you want the truth that hurts now..?

Katie finished the line, "Or a lie that will hurt later? Okay, give it to me straight."

"He has been seeing someone else."

∗

Later that afternoon, Jean walked Katie around the rest of the farm. It was huge and they didn't get even get down as far as the fields facing out towards Holcot Village.

There were seven huge barns and sheds around the main farmyard. All but two, one which stored the feed and the other machinery, housed animals of one kind or another. Katie had accepted that there would be chickens, goats and the odd pony but, in reality, there were far more animals than she could have possibly imagined. Animals ranging from pot-bellied pigs, orphaned lambs, guinea pigs and even a turkey called Tina.

"Goodness," Katie declared, "I had no idea places like this even existed." She gently stroked the head of one of the lambs. "Where's its mother?"

"Who knows?" said Jean, "Sometimes the mother dies or rejects them. With multiple births, the mother often can't feed all of them."

"Ah, I see." The lamb was really cute and kept on nudging Katie to keep on stroking it. "How do they get here then?" The lamb sucked at her fingers, prompting Katie to pull her hand away.

"Everyone in Devon knew Liza would take in whatever wasn't loved. Because she loved them all." Lovely Liza again.

"She'd get a call, day or night, and she'd always take them in."

"But how could she afford it? How does the farm make enough money to cover the cost of their feed?"

"Oh, don't ask me." Jean replied. "I just do what I'm told. Leave the thinking to others."

Clearly Katie was going to have to do a lot of thinking. Thinking and learning.

But first, she was going to have to wash her hands.

Chapter eight

For the next few days, Katie found herself dusting, washing and generally being more active than she'd ever been. She knew deep down it was all a diversionary tactic to keep Oliver and his secret life out of her thoughts. Katie had an inner voice that never shut off, particularly when it came to dwelling on things which she either regretted or found sad. She had a really bad habit of tormenting herself.
 Her mother had once told her after a nasty break up of her own, "if you're sad -keep busy" whilst she repeatedly bleached her own kitchen cupboards and sobbed about the "scoundrel" who had "done the dirty." Amazing that Katie now used some of her mother's mantras after years of swearing blind that she would never be anything like her mother.
She had to admit it though, after watching a few You Tube videos of energetic women clearing out their

houses whilst giving them an all-over deep clean, Katie had become quite invested in getting the farmhouse looking ship-shape again. It was a charming building and would make a lovely family home for someone if, and when, she finally came to sell it. She found that she was actually starting to enjoy the whole cleaning process – it felt somehow honest and purifying.

She worked on clearing one room at a time, covers and throws were aired, beds were bashed and spiders prised from their havens. Jean helpfully took some old cushions home to sew and repair and between them, and the ever-effervescent Maisie, there was a sense of a new beginning. The scent of mould and decay replaced with that of clean linen and lavender.

*

Katie decided it was time to tackle Liza's bedroom next, she could only sleep on the sofa for so long. Women's bedrooms are such personal spaces that she felt it intrusive just to go in and take a look around. Whether the house was going to be sold or demolished Katie needed to sort out Liza's personal belongings. She was really hoping for the former but knew that, realistically, the latter was much more likely.

The room, the master bedroom, was musty and functional. Old heavy brocade curtains hung, unloved and tatty, down from the windows of the dual aspect bedroom. Lace net curtains, probably quite lovely when they were first put up, hung grey and lifeless within their huge square frames.

She began by climbing onto a stool, which looked like a piano stool, so that she could unhook the textiles before dropping them onto the floor. As soon as she'd done it, she realised she'd made a mistake as a thick cloud of dust motes rose up to greet her, making her cough and splutter.

She started opening the windows as wide as she could even though some of them were stiff and wedged shut with age. She worried about breaking a pane with the force she needed to use in order to crack them open but decided that the risk was worth it. When she was finished, she got down off the stool and was rewarded with a blast of cool, fresh air which seemed to sweep everything aside, exposing the room to a new level of scrutiny.

With her hands on her hips, she slowly surveyed what remained of Aunt Liza's room.

The furniture was clearly very old, dark brown heavy wood. The bed itself had carved wooden legs and the headboard was enormous. As she moved in to examine it more closely, the random patterns that she had previously thought were on it turned out to be a detailed carving of some rural idyllic scene containing sheep and trees. Katie took a damp cloth and wiped the residual dust away. What emerged was beautifully detailed and had clearly been carved by hand.

She definitely wouldn't have room for something like

that in her flat, so she'd have to sell it. Sell Aunt Liza's bed. This all felt too personal. Under the bed, Katie discovered a handmade wooden box which she pulled open to reveal wads of black and white photographs, slips of paper, letters and old used cinema and concert tickets. She'd look through those later.

Liza had acquired some beautiful pieces of antique furniture that just needed curating and Katie was curious about where they'd all come from. Had her grandparents once owned these things? It was impossible to know. What on earth was she going to do with all this stuff when it was time to leave?

Katie continued around the room, there was no way she could clean it all today and – goodness - she was definitely going to need a fresh supply of cleaning materials.

She was going to have to clear out the drawers and the wardrobe. She didn't really want to but she was the only surviving family member Liza still had. She'd have to make it work somehow. Katie decided to begin with the wardrobe. What would be in there? There was a large ornate brass key sitting in the lock. She didn't need to turn it however as the wardrobe handle pivoted downwards easily on a first go and the door sprang open.

There were a few jackets and skirts hanging inside and one long, plastic covered garment. Katie noticed some old leather high heel shoes at the bottom along with a pair of tennis shoes.

As she pushed the line of hangers back and removed the garment, she began to see what it was. She draped it over the bed, gasping in delight as she began to open the zipper. There, in a blaze of white silk was a wedding dress. She marvelled at the intricacy of the bodice as she stripped away the grey plastic sheath. And what she was left with made her heart cry out. "Oh Liza, what have you left me?" Katie exclaimed.

*

That night, Katie slept in Liza's bed. She couldn't quite believe what was happening to her. It was like going on an archaeological retreat only to realise that everything you'd discovered linked back in some way to your own family tree. She was meant to be going back to London in a few days with all her family commitments neatly wrapped up, but how was that ever going to happen after all this to contend with? She felt that she needed to learn as much as she could about the farm and its workings so that she'd be in a better position when it came to sell it. Could it perhaps be sold as an animal sanctuary? She guessed you'd have to be pretty mad to buy something that was so difficult to maintain and was almost guaranteed to make a loss no matter how hard you worked at it. Still, she had to focus on the positive. There was an asset here somewhere. She'd just have to get it valued and hope for the best.

She was woken by the sound of scaping coming from downstairs. It was not quite morning. What on earth could it be? This was followed by a loud bang and the sound of someone moving about in the kitchen. She slid into her Cuppini slippers and headed off to investigate. When she reached the hallway, she removed a long umbrella from the stand. Then, raising it above her head, she began moving towards the kitchen.

In the half light, she could just make out someone, bent over, shuffling around. They seemed to be looking for something and the back door was wide open.

She could hear the sound of her blood pulsing in her ears.

"Get out! Right now! I've called the police and they're on their way!"

Rounding the table she saw a pair of eyes looking straight back up at her. A pig, a massive pot-bellied pig, stood snuffling at a baking tray that she'd used the night before to make a Victoria sponge cake. Now, there was virtually nothing left. She released a breath she hadn't known she'd been holding and fell back onto the sofa. The pig continued to snaffle the last of the crumbs. In his own time, he turned and headed for the door, giving Katie one last dismissive look.

"This is never going to work!" she wailed, dropping the umbrella down onto the sofa while resolving that she had to hire a farm manager as soon as possible.

*

Katie was on her knees scrubbing the quarry tiles by the Aga. Everything was physically more demanding than she had been expecting. Everything. She often woke to aches in muscles that she never even knew that she had. Meanwhile, Jean was using newspaper and vinegar to clean the windows, much to Katie's bemusement.

"Oh Katie, the old-fashioned ways are often still the best," Jean mused,

"Ah, actually, not when it comes to things like dentistry and modern medicine," Katie retorted trying to score points in their mini debate.

"We really must get the top field sorted out," Jean mused. "Farmer Baker's Herefords have been grazing up there and it all needs managing."

All the time Jean was talking, Katie was smiling as she watched Maisie, out in the pens, feeding the piglets. There was much squawking and hilarity as the ten or so piglets barged one another aside in their attempts to get more food from Maisie's bucket.

"Jean, I think those top fields are supposed to be where the Highways Agency plans to start building if they get approval. It's not be worth investing any more time into them until we find out."

"And what then? Will they flatten the rest of the farm and the farmhouse as well?

"I really don't know," Katie said, wringing her cloth out into the bucket. "I'm assuming they'll want it all, though. All the land."

"It doesn't seem fair that they can do that- just force you out of your home 'cos it suits them." Jean pushed open the window. "Maisie Jane! That's enough! Now, let them be."

"It's not my home though, Jean, is it?"

"No, I s'pose not," she said, pulling the window shut. "But it's not theirs neither."

Katie paused. Jean was right, this was their home, at least for now. And Katie was suddenly struck by a real sense of her own responsibilities. In the past, she'd never had to consider anyone else's interests other than her own and she was finding this difficult. Katie poured the dirty water into the sink and stopped to watch the dark brown water slowly drain away. "Look, why don't we plant out anyway, even if it is temporary. What is it we're actually having to sort out? A crop, something fast growing?"

Jean's spirits lifted, "Oh no, just Wild Thyme and Marjoram, we need to manage the scrub around them."

Katie looked quizzical.

"It's for the butterflies," Jean explained. "Liza said she'd neglected the field for far too long and that they'd never come back if it wasn't done this year. The conservation bloke fella said it's the only way that Swedish caterpillars can survive."

"Conservation fella? Swedish caterpillars?"

"Nice man, visited last year. Bit obsessed."

Katie grimaced, did she really want to be bothered with butterflies when, within the year, a huge digger might be churning up their habitat? But then, she'd be gone by then anyway and it would be down to whoever bought the farm to manage it.

"I'll get the tools onto the trailer for later," Jean said, smiling. And then, before Katie could change her mind, she disappeared out the back door, leaving Katie, shaking her head.

Chapter nine

Just as Katie was about to climb up into the Land Rover next to Jean, James Baker appeared.

"Afternoon ladies," he said, taking in the metal trailer they'd spent the last ten minutes connecting to the back of the Land Rover. "And where are you two lovelies off to? "

Jean was clearly thrilled to see him. "James, we're going up to the top field to lay out Thyme and Marjoram. Want to come?"

"I certainly would."

Without saying anything, he took Katie's arm and helped her clamber into the middle seat. Then he climbed up beside her before closing the door. He seemed ridiculously big sitting next to Katie, pressing her up against the far side of her seat.

He pointed down at her feet, "Nice boots!" he laughed, prompting Jean to snort conspiratorially.

"What's wrong with them?" Katie loved her pink Hunter wellies.

"Don't get many pink wellingtons down this way, that's all," he said, smiling sweetly.

"I'll get you a pair," she joked.

"It's okay. Don't trouble yourself. Anyway, how are you getting on? Katherine, is it? Or Katie?" he continued to smile down at her as Jean drove out into the far lane and along beside the metal sheds. They hurtled along with the metal trailer bouncing around at the back making Katie feeling quite breathless.

"Yes," she sighed. "Good, quite good. Just getting settled."

"Really? So, you're getting settled in then?"

"Well not settling per se. Just until the farm is sold."

James nodded and turned to look out over the fields.

"Of course. I hear you're looking for a farm manager – that'll be expensive if you're gonna let the farm go. I could help you if you needed some help."

Jean looked across at James and smiled. "Oh, James that would be so nice- we really do need a man to help with some of the jobs."

"Do we?" Katie exclaimed, she did not like having to admit that she needed help from anyone, let alone a man.

"Yes, we need all the stuff in the shed shifting."

There was silence between them. Katie reflected on the situation and looked up into James' face. He had a very kind face.

Perhaps she just needed to learn how to relax.

"Thank you, that would be very kind, James "

Finally he smiled.

*

It had turned into a beautifully bright afternoon, warm and colourful. It hadn't been until they'd got to the top farm that Katie realised that James had agreed to come with them in order to check on his father's Herefords. He wandered away from them, through the long grass, heading to the very top of the field where the cows stood regally surveying the fields around them.

She caught herself thinking that James looked like a magnificent animal in his own right and had to stop herself from getting carried away. Get a grip, she thought.

"Over here," Jean called.

Jean took a couple of shovels out of the back of the Land Rover and handed one to Katie. "We need to try to get rid of as much scrub as possible around those plants."

Katie was having difficulty making out the difference between the scrub and the plants themselves. She'd never been able to keep a houseplant alive for longer than two weeks, so this was really going to be a challenge.

Jean saw her confusion. "See, this here, with the start of the blue buds, this is thyme. The butterflies love to lay their eggs here. It's where their whole life cycle begins."

"I remember reading something about this at school"

"Actually, Jean," James boomed, striding over. "I think you've missed the grown-up part of how the eggs get made in the first place."

Jean hurried away, "Oh, you do know how to embarrass an old woman." She hurried off to their left and started digging out a shallow ditch in front of the bank of thyme.

James reached for Katie's shovel.

"It's fine. I can manage," she retorted, moving over in Jean's direction and beginning to force her shovel into the unyielding earth. She tried her best to copy Jean's efforts but, within a couple of minutes, she was already struggling.

She was aware of James watching her in amusement and decided she had to redouble her efforts.

He reached into the back of the Land Rover and removed a garden fork. It somehow looked small in his hands. He proceeded to turn the earth over at terrific pace as if it was an Olympic sport. Katie stood there trying not to look impressed but he was – well - very impressed.

As the hours went by there were occasional opportunities for them to stop for water and to admire their handiwork. Katie felt part of something.

"When are you going back to London, Katie?" James asked openly.

In the background, Katie saw Jean stiffen. She was desperate to know what was going on.

"Not for a while I don't think. I've asked if I can take a 6-month sabbatical. I think they might be sympathetic to it now. You see, I've just been passed over for promotion, so my whole life's in a bit of turmoil."

"Wont someone be missing you back there? In London?"

Katie smiled. "Are you trying to ask if I have a boyfriend?"

"I might be," he replied, sheepishly

"No. There's no one back there for me now."

They continued digging in silence as the sun began to dip towards the horizon.

Jean suddenly started striding off in the direction of the Land Rover.

"Right, ho!" she said, throwing her spade into the back of the trailer. "Why don't I take this back to the farm and get some dinner on. James, you could walk Katie back and show her the perimeter of the farm."

"Katie?"

"I really would like to see it all properly."

He took Katie's spade from her and placed them carefully in the trailer. Jean smiled as if she had a secret and set off with a knowing look, glancing back as the two of them as they fell into step along the lane.

"So, let me get this straight," Katie said. "We have to provide a suitable environment for the butterflies to complete their life cycle. To allow a certain number to thrive."

"Yes, it's been decades since there were butterflies on the farm. It was always great regret on Liza's part and she was determined to put it right. The Big Blue apparently became extinct across the whole country sometime in the seventies. She got in touch with some conservation people who told her how to go about it. Even the Herefords being up here is part of the plan."

"Really? This is all starting make more sense. I did have a letter from a Mr. Carruthers asking about the hedgerows. But if it's not a bill I haven't had time to deal with it. But I'll write to him now. Let him know what's happening to the farm."

"Farm's in trouble then?"

"Very much so I'm afraid. If the Highways Agency don't come up with the cash I'm going to have to sell it anyway, as soon as the year is up. The income doesn't bring in enough to even cover the cost of the feed."

"How did Liza manage it, then?"

"She didn't. When she died, she had virtually nothing left. From what I gather although she has Tumbledown Cottage, she'd mortgaged the farm. I'm not going to be a millionairess any time soon."

"Unless the Highways Agency…"

"Exactly."

There was a gentle moment of silence as they walked side by side.

"Do you remember that field over there - near our orchard. When we were kids, I remember building our den there and playing house, building a fire and melting all that chocolate."

She laughed fondly. "Burning it, more like."

"I was devastated when you just, disappeared one day. Never returned. I found out from Liza that you and your mother had gone back to the city. She was completely devastated after you'd gone."

"I know. I remember it all. There was a lot of shouting that day." Katie tapped into the painful memory of her mother standing there in tears, saying that she was never coming back. "You were my first proper friend."

"Boyfriend?"

She smiled at the memory. "Okay. Yes, boyfriend."

As they came across the brow of the hill and could see the farmhouse, James turned to her.

"Katie, if you're going to leave and go back to London…" he hesitated and for a moment she sensed his vulnerability. "It's probably best for all of us, if you go sooner rather than later."

She shook her head.

"I can't live here, James, I just can't. I don't know anything about this life. I like the city, I belong there.

69

I like bars and restaurants and - I don't know - people. I've got a career."

As she said it out loud she found herself thinking: but is that really true? How many people did she actually like in London? How many bars did she really enjoy drinking in these days? Wasn't all that just a lot of hype? A way of camouflaging how she truly felt? Isolated and alone.

"I understand," he said. "And that's exactly why I couldn't live anywhere other than here. I belong here. But I just hope you realise that if you do sell to the Highways Agency our land will also be affected. Your life will go on, you may well earn a pretty penny out of all this. But, as for the rest of us, we'll end up paying a very heavy price."

"I don't understand."

"We can't afford to carry on milking cows so close to a complex road system. It just wouldn't be practical. The farm will be rendered almost worthless as a result. In the end, we'd probably end up having to sell up ourselves." He looked at his boots, "Your decision will have a huge impact on all the farms round here, Katherine. But the biggest losers will be us, your direct neighbours. "

Katherine had not thought about any of these implications and it was coming as something of a shock. He was clearly sad and a not a little angry about the situation he found himself in. "You can't just hand it all over to the Highways Agency. They'd

70

ruin us."

She got the distinct impression that she was being cornered, and that Jean might have been complicit in arranging all this.

"You're suggesting that I've got more influence on this that I actually have," she explained. "But I won't have a choice if the agency decides to press ahead."

James snorted his frustration.

The kitchen door opened as they crossed the yard.

"Right, you two. Dinner?" Jean said in a sing-song voice, drying her hands on a tea towel.

"I won't be stopping," James said firmly before striding off and out the front gate.

Katie watched him go.

"Katie?"

She held up her hand. "Just don't ask."

Chapter ten

The clean-up of the house continued with Katie trying to keep abreast of all the creditors that were currently pursuing the estate.

Her experience as a lawyer was more than useful in negotiating repayments and dealing directly with people in positions of authority and she was quietly encouraged by their positive response to her current predicament. She had explained the whole situation of the inheritance to everyone the farm owed money to, leaving them in no doubt that in one way or another it would be sold within the year, whether that be to the Highways Agency or to new owners. They would all get their money, with interest. She was presently living on her own savings.

She had been rocked though by James' outburst about the farm and the effect it might have on the

Bakers' family. She could understand what he was saying but it wasn't her fault that things were going in that direction. It was largely out of her hands. She would try to control and manage what she could in the interim but ultimately The Highways Agency were the ones in the driving seat.

Simon Martindale rang her late one evening. "Katherine, Farmer Katherine," she could hear the sarcasm in his voice. "Darling girl, just to let you know that we're all still here. Enjoying your sabbatical? Sophie La Cruz has picked up your work and is doing a great job. Glad we've got her on board." He caught himself, "Of course, we're all missing you!"

Funny, Katie thought, I haven't missed you at all.

At Butterfly Farm itself they were all settling down to a gentle pattern of getting-on-with-things and Jean and Maisie were constant, though very welcome guests - they just never considered the idea that Katie might want to be on her own every once in a while. It helped that they were such excellent company. Every night while Jean sewed next to the crackling fire, Maisie would read her Princess Diaries book to them, doing all the voices and making them laugh hysterically.

Jean had tried to ensure that everything carried on for the animals pretty much as normal. Feed was ordered and was readily available and she worked tirelessly every day. When it came to keeping everything running as efficiently as possible, Jean was an invaluable companion.

The animals themselves seemed happy enough and Katie actually enjoyed checking on them late at night on her own after the others had gone home. There was a stillness to the farm at that time as, with an empty bucket in one hand, she stood next to the pig pen and looked up to the empty sky. For the first time, she saw nothing but stars, black sky and sparkling stars. It was an incredibly humbling experience. Perhaps this peaceful farm had more to offer than Katie had originally thought.

But was she fooling herself when she fancied that one day she might be able to run the place on her own? At that precise moment, Prince, a pot belly pig kicked out and sent a bucket flying into Katie's leg, covering her with muck and making her cry out.

"Ow!" she shouted, rubbing her knee. "Thanks for the vote of confidence!"

*

Katie was determined to do her best for the farm while she was still there.

"Jean?" she probed, after breakfast. "Do you think you could show me how Liza ran the farm, day to day I mean. I'd really like to get a feel for the actual flow of resources and logistics."

"Oh," Jean replied, washing her hands. "Resources and logistics is it?" she laughed. "Really, it's not that complicated, just gotta work hard, all day long."

"But I need to work out how and where the farm gets its money from and how it's meant to be spent if I'm going to have any chance of straightening it out before it gets sold. I've got to work out if it's possible to make the farm turn a profit."

"Right, I get you. Well, Liza kept the money stuff quiet, I didn't even know there was a problem until she died. Then, of course, we went cap in hand to a few animal charities to keep us going until you arrived."

"Okay, because if the Highways Agency doesn't end up buying it we need to be able to present the place as a going. Do you understand?"

"Yes, I think so."

"Right, time to get into the minutiae then."

"Ok," said Jean. "Let's start with the minutiae of mucking out the sheds."

They both chuckled.

*

Three of the farm outbuildings had animals in them of all types and breeds while over in one corner, the pigs and piglets were very happily housed in their muddy pens.

"We'll be moving them to the outdoor pens soon," said Jean indicating the goats and pigs. "They enjoy the grass lands."

"Do you milk the goats?" asked Katie.

"No, these are meat goats."

"Really? But we're not selling them for meat are we?"

Jean laughed, "No. Round here we sell them almost as pets to manage the fields and hedgerows."

The range of horses in the far shed was almost comical. A large, heavily built horse snuggled up alongside two ponies, one which was tiny in stature.

"That's Jimmy, Flash and the miniature is Tinkerbell. They go out every day into the fields but we do need to keep an eye on Tinker, she can nip and be a bit nasty." Jean pushed up her sleeve to reveal an old but significant scar high on her forearm. "She must have been having a bad day. She came from a troubled home. When we first got her, she was unkempt and completely uncared for."

Katie pulled a shocked face, she couldn't see herself being quite so philosophical about an injury like that.

"So, she says she loves you with a nip?"

"Yes, she even nipped Mr. Willis, the vet"

Vet's bills, something else to add to Katie's growing list of outgoings.

Katie spent some time going over all of the feed in the feed shed, even though Jean had enjoyed telling her that she might come across a rat or two. The shed was only about a quarter full and it didn't take long for Katie to realise that feed was seriously dwindling.

"This will last about another week, week and a half at most," Jean said, forlornly.

"How much do we need, Jean? How much money, approximately, each week?"

Jean mused, "I don't know, really. I just order and the

bill comes to the house. I don't know how much we pay."

Katie's brain started firing, "Right, tell me who you ring and about how much you order each week."

"I've got the details written down indoors."

Katie was clearly frustrated with the lack of detail. Jean went quiet whilst they moved behind some hay bales. "I've done my best Katie, really I have."

Katie realised that she was being harsh and gently took hold of Jean by the shoulders so she could look directly at her. "Jean, you have done brilliantly. These animals are still alive because of you. You! And we are going to keep them healthy and well looked after. We just need to work out how to raise the money to keep feeding them, that's all. "

"Resources and logistics?" Jean said.

"Exactly!"

*

Late on there was a knock on the kitchen door. It startled Katie.

"Hello," came a voice. "It's me, James."

Katie smoothed her hair away from her face and quickly pinched her cheeks, though a little too hard. She unlocked the door and opened it.

"James? It's very late."

"I know," he said, coming through the door. Then he paused, "Are you ok?"

"Yes, of course, why?"

"Your cheeks. They look really red."

Katie was suddenly embarrassed. "Oh I'm fine." She looked around for an excuse and then said, falteringly, "Been sitting too close to the fire, that's all."

They both turned to the fire which was just a black cold mess. He frowned.

"Earlier," she said, wanting to move on. "It was hot earlier. Anyway, what can I do for you?"

"Just wondering if you wanted to watch a calf being born?"

"Now?"

"Yes, the cow needs a caesarean and the vet's on his way."

"Caesarean, as in 'cut-out' the calf? Oh I don't know if I ..."

"Why don't you come and see. If you don't like the look of it, you can come straight back."

*

Navigating her way across the muddied tracks between the farms had been quite perilous and more than once James had taken her arm to steady her. Years of tractor traffic had taken its toll on the unmade road.

The barn they entered looked almost biblical in nature, Katie thought. Luckily, the evening was reasonably warm and the large barn had numerous lights in the far corner near a huge column of hay bales stacked one on top of the other.

There was some movement and noise up ahead as James guided her towards where the action was.

"Try and be quiet so we don't frighten her," James said.

The cow stood, calm, tethered by a rope to a metal rail. Katie thought how big it was close up and for a moment was a little afraid as it turned its head to get a better look at these newcomers.

The vet, Mr. Willis, turned and smiled at Katie. He was almost completely protected by a long, plastic apron and wellington boots. He had already washed the whole of the cow's swollen stomach with some kind of pink coloured antiseptic and was about to set to work with a large scalpel.

Katie took a deep breath and turned nervously to James who nodded his reassurance that everything was going to be ok.

The next few minutes were other-worldly. The cow must have had an anaesthetic of some kind as she seemed calm and untroubled throughout. The cut was placed vertically and deeply. There was blood, but nothing like Katie would have expected.

The vet put his hands inside the open wound and began to manoeuvre the calf out through the stomach wall.

"Come on now," he whispered.

There was lots of pushing and shoving for about a minute, his hands, deep inside the cow now, were moving firmly but purposefully.

And then, almost magically, he pulled a long dark shape out through the wound and dragged it across the floor.

It was a slimy mess but Katie could make out little black and white legs in a translucent bag. James stepped forward at that point, helping to drag the calf towards one of the warming lights. He ripped away the thin sticky bag from around the calf's snout before he began rubbing its body frenetically with some straw.

Katie didn't know quite what was happening but knew that as far as the calf was concerned, this was a pivotal moment.

Seconds seemed to drag by like minutes.

"Try the snout," Willis said and James unceremoniously twisted the snout towards his own mouth before he started blowing air into it, hard. Was he clearing the airway? Katie didn't know but whatever he was doing she knew that something had to happen, and quick.

Willis began to move across to the unfolding scene. Suddenly the calf moved independently, a twitch initially, and then it moved its head. James released the animal's jaw, spitting to one side before continuing to rub the body with the straw, in an attempt to stimulate the lungs.

"It's alright, she's alright, "James smiled and instantly the tension was broken.

He sat back on his heels triumphantly, looking

straight at Katie who found herself crying and
laughing, both at the same time.

Chapter eleven

"Oh Katie!" Lucy shot out of the driving seat and threw herself into Katie's arms. "I've missed you so much. It's been months."

Katie hugged Lucy hard, feeling their deep friendship moulding them together.

"Lucy! Oh, Lucy you look great!" Katie stood back so that she could look at her. "What have you been doing?"

"Never mind me, what about you? All this?" and she ranged her eyes around the farm.

"I know, mad isn't it?"

They both laughed and then, after another hug, they headed off the farmhouse to catch up.

Within the hour they'd drunk a bottle of prosecco while Lucy had spilled the beans on her developing relationship with Daniel, the environmental lawyer.

Then she told her how the Wellbeing Weekend had worked out. It seemed to have been particularly good for Lucy's own wellbeing since she had been ended up being kissed by the sasquatch.

"Trouble is, I really like him."

"How can that be trouble?"

"All men are trouble."

"Ain't that the truth," Katie poured herself another drink. "Oliver has stopped texting, finally."

She went to the mantel piece and took down the ring that he had given her. "How am I going to get this back to him?"

She placed it down on the table.

Lucy considered the ring, sparkling forlornly.

"Actually, Katie, I wouldn't worry about it."

"But it's a family heirloom – his grandmother gave it to him."

"Yes, well, don't waste your time worrying about him. I don't mean to be cruel, but I don't think he's given you much thought."

That cut Katie. Although she knew it was over, deep down she wanted him to have been left devasted by their separation and regretful about what he'd done. How he'd come to lose her.

"That was a bit harsh," she said.

"Not really. You see that woman he was seeing. Well, she's pregnant."

*

After a late night sharing every story they possibly could Katie came down late the next morning with a thick head. She found Lucy sitting in the kitchen, bright eyed and bushy tailed, getting stuck into a plate of eggs on toast while Jean watched from the range. "Morning," Katie sat down opposite Maisie who was adding up the money she had made from that week's egg sales.

"I like money," she stated, boldly.

"Me too," replied Lucy, folding some eggs into her mouth while making an approving face. "Perhaps you can show me how you collect and size the eggs? Katie says you're an expert at it."

Maisie blushed and looked down, "Not an expert" she said humbly, "but I do like chickens. And they don't mind me taking their eggs. They're proud to show me them sometimes."

Lucy went to say something, but Maisie cut in. "Once I had an egg and it was as big as my hand!" She held up her hand to reinforce the size.

"Gosh, I bet that chicken had tears in her eyes," Lucy quipped.

"No, silly they don't cry, they're animals!"

And Lucy, suitably chastised, smiled, nodded and returned to her breakfast.

"So, Miss Katie will you both be going to Liza's 'do' tonight?" asked Jean, pouring Katie a glass of water and dropping two painkillers next to it on the table.

"Of course! That's tonight isn't it?" she turned to

84

Lucy. "You will come won't you Lucy?"

"I haven't brought anything to dress up in!"

"Oh you won't have to worry about that," said Jean. "Most of the village will be coming in late from the fields so we'll be lucky if the men have even had a wash."

Lucy raised an eyebrow at that before turning to Katie. "And will Mr. Baker be there?"

Jean replied, "Not old Mr. Baker, no, he's not been well for years. That's why James has had to carry on running the business for him."

It was the first time that Katie had heard about this. She had been so caught up with her own life she hadn't considered anybody else's troubles. No wonder James was never going to leave. He couldn't. Not really.

"But I'd be surprised if the young 'uns don't go," Jean said. "We like a knees up in the village, we do."

"Then yes, I'd love to meet your neighbours, Katie," Lucy said, giving her a knowing wink.

*

Katie and Lucy knocked at the door of Tumbledown cottage at the end of the lane.

"I feel really odd wearing a dress," Katie remarked, brushing down the front of her blue and white tea dress. "I don't think I've seen anyone's legs since I've been here."

"Oh, Katie, you look lovely," Lucy said. And she did. She was wearing her dark, brunette hair down for once and had brushed the curls into a swathe down over her right shoulder. With her blue eyes and pale face her colouring was eye catching. "Will you have to make a speech or anything?"

"What! No!" Katie was not happy with that suggestion.

The door opened and Jean and Maisie bustled out, grabbing last minute cardigans and handbags.

"Maisie you look lovely," Katie said. "Look at your lovely long skirt." Maisie had a long black skirt that had three butterflies sewn around the waistband.

"And I've got lipstick on!" she pouted at Lucy. "Nan said I'm beautiful."

Jean moved onto the pavement and turned to lock the door. "And you are, my darling girl. But remember what I said, no naughty drinking, not even one."

"I like coca cola anyway."

The four made their way two by two along the high street to the White Horse pub.

"Jean, I just wanted to …"

"Yes?"

"Thank you. Thank you, for looking for me. For looking after all of us."

"Oh, I don't know any other way!" she said, though she was clearly touched.

"You really don't have to cook for me every

morning."

"You keep buying the food and I'll keep doing the cooking," Jean gave Katie's arm a squeeze. "You're doing alright, Katie. Liza would be proud."

Katie smiled appreciatively.

"Shall we go in?"

The lights of a disco were already spilling out through the pub windows and into the street with "Come on Eileen" booming over the speakers.

They opened the door and stepped inside.

*

Katie spotted James straight away, she could hardly miss him. His huge frame was holding up the far end of the bar and he had his head thrown back and was laughing. He was clearly enjoying the company around him and Katie felt a pang of jealousy as she noticed one of them was a small pretty woman with tousled blonde hair and hazel eyes. Attractive.

"Jean, Maisie, let me get you ladies a drink," Katie began to usher Lucy ahead of her towards the bar. Jean called out after them, "We'll try and get a table, shall we?" before moving towards the rear of the pub.

"Is that him? "Lucy leaned into Katie's ear. "Please, tell me that's him."

And as Katie nodded her agreement, Lucy opened her mouth in shocked approval.

The pub was full and as Katie took her place at the

bar, people turned to her to say hello.

"Well, hello again, Miss Katie," the barman said and it took her a moment to realise that it was Mr. Riley, all spruced up with his hair combed to one side.

"What can I get you?"

"My, Mr. Riley, you look very handsome this evening," he nodded in agreement.

"This is my friend, Lucy. Lucy, what are we drinking?"

"Hmmm," she pursed her lips looking along the length of the bar. "I'm thinking Espresso Martini." Katie gave Mr. Riley an indulgent smile.

"Well, Miss Lucy you can think that while you're drink something we actually have in. Wine, beer, spirits?"

"Ah!" Lucy realised her small-town faux pas. "Righto, I'll have a glass of white wine please."

"Sweet or dry?"

"Any other choices?"

"Nope."

Katie stepped in, "Two dry white wines, a coke and ..." she realised she had no idea what Jean would be drinking.

Suddenly a large, bearded face loomed over her.

"Jean likes a whisky." It was James. He smelt wonderful: fresh, yet still earthy.

"Thank you, James. And what would you like?"

"No thank you, I've got a beer," and he raised his pint glass, dwarfed by his huge hand, by way of a salute.

As Mr. Riley got on with pouring the drinks, Katie introduced James to Lucy.

"This is my friend, Lucy. Lucy, James Baker, my neighbour."

"Hello, pleased to meet you," Lucy said. "I've heard a lot about you."

Katie squinted at her in mock admonishment.

"Have you really? "

The three of them stood rather awkwardly.

"Right, well, I'll take these over," said Lucy scooting off with the first two drinks, easing her way through the crowd.

"How have you been?" James asked.

"Actually, I did want to talk to you about something."

There was something unspoken that went between them at that moment. An attraction that was palpable. As James bent down so that he could hear her better, Katie caught her breath.

"James, I," she was struggling to communicate properly. "I was wondering if you would help me do some work, with the brick outbuilding."

He eased himself back into a more upright position and smiled to himself as if to say, 'I should have known'.

"Yes," Katie reassured herself that she was functioning again. "I'm thinking about plans for selling and we could get more for it if we make that a suitable place for a business. Office space. You know

89

the kind of thing?

He replied slowly, "Yes, I know the kind of thing. Later. Let's discuss this later."

Katie was about to say something but he interrupted her.

"We're here to remember how much effort Liza put into the farm, rather than how much we can make out of it."

And, clearly disapproving, he made his way back to the blonde woman at the end of the bar.

Katie was wounded. She had been insensitive and crass. Even her embarrassment at being so close to someone she was so obviously attracted to could not forgive such a thoughtless comment at a time like this.

She made her way over to the corner table Jean had acquired and sat down with a heavy heart.

*

She stayed sitting in the corner for the rest of the night while everyone else seemed to be having a high old time. By ten thirty, Maisie had found her dancing legs, had had one coca cola too many and was wheeling around to Abba's Dancing Queen. Jean laughed and clapped alongside her. Lucy was chatting to the locals along the bar. She seemed to be quizzing them about something and was very interested in their replies.

Katie looked forlornly over at James. He seemed a little more subdued than he had been earlier, though the blonde woman appeared to be on good form. Henry, James' brother, was also in the bar and, when he saw Katie, he waved. She brightened for a moment and waved back.

Then the speeches began. Mr. Riley clumsily shouting at the DJ to turn the music down before ringing the bell over the bar. At first, Katie thought that he was ringing for last orders and it was only then that she realised that she had been steadily drinking all evening. But no, it was clear by the way that Mr Riley took his place at the microphone that he had something to say.

"Thank you all for coming tonight," he began. "Liza, as you know, has charged our glasses this evening and put on one last show for us all to enjoy. "

This was met with a general whoop of approval. "She was a wonderful woman, always thinking of others. And, she could really hold her ale!"

Cheering

"I'd like to welcome Katie, Liza's niece, properly to the village."

Eyes turned in Katie's direction prompting her to nod her head in acknowledgement.

"We are sure she will do what is right for the farm, for the village and for Liza."

Katie raised her glass to that while Mr Riley carried on, telling a funny story about Liza and a runaway pig at Christmas. Everyone seemed to have the story before but that didn't stop them laughing in all the right places.

After one final story, he finished by cajoling everyone to give three cheers in Liza's memory, the response all but raising the roof. Then it was the DJ's turn to encourage people to get up and dance by playing Neil Diamond's "Sweet Caroline." Lucy got straight up and tried to encourage Katie to join her but had to make-do with a spin around the dancefloor with Jean. Katie took her opportunity and slipped off to the toilets to escape. She needed some space. She wished she'd never come. Never come to this village. She sat alone in a cubicle for a while until, finally, she realised that she couldn't stay there indefinitely. She stepped out of the cubicle and made her way over to the taps. After flicking water on her face, she raised her head and stared at her own reflection - who even was she? What the hell was she doing here anyway? She stood up, straightening her dress. No. She wasn't going to start feeling bad about offending someone she hardly even knew. She didn't owe Liza anything. It wasn't Katie's fault that she'd chosen to leave the farm to her.

As she made her way along the narrow corridor back towards the main bar, she came across James. The way that he was standing, he was completely blocking the way, making it obvious that he was waiting to speak to her.

"Katie."

She drew a deep breath and mentally donned her

armour. Was he about to chastise her again; she wasn't going to stand for it. Not this time.

Because of the noise from the bar, he had to bend forward to make himself heard.

"Would it really be so bad to live here, at Dunsford? Really? "

This was not what she'd been expecting. She looked up at him, confused. "I don't understand. Here? What is there here for me?"

He paused while considering his reply. Then he reached out and gently took her by the arms.

"Me?"

When he pulled her to him, she didn't resist and, suddenly, she was eight years old again, standing at the farm gate.

She kept her eyes closed while they kissed, surrendering herself completely to the moment.

Next thing, they heard the sound of voices coming along the corner. Two women heading for the Ladies'.

Startled, they pulled away from one another, like teenagers who'd been caught making out. They pressed themselves awkwardly up against the wall, allowing the two women enough room to pass them by. It perhaps wouldn't have been so bad if Katie hadn't recognised one of them as the small blonde from earlier.

As she made her way down the corridor, the woman turned and gave James a knowing smile. Katie couldn't help wondering who she might be. What their connection was.

Returning to her table, now with a skip in her step, Katie heard the opening chords of Whitney Houston's "Million-Dollar Bill." Taking Maisie by the hand, she pulled her to her feet before manoeuvring her towards the dancefloor, where Jean and Lucy were waiting.

"Where did you disappear off to?" Lucy shouted Lucy over the sound of the singing.

Katie turned to look at James who was now back at the bar. Their eyes met and she couldn't help but smile.

Chapter twelve

There was a ring at the doorbell. Early morning.
Katie was about to head out to join Maisie in feeding
the new donkey. It had arrived as an emergency the
day before. The RSPCA had rung up, begging Katie
to take it in temporarily while they tried to rehome it.
It was a scared but stubborn thing which Jean and
Katie had managed to coax into a spare pen, in the
corner opposite the pigs. She wanted to see how he'd
coped sleeping in his first shelter for years. Katie had
just been putting on her Barbour jacket when the
doorbell rang.

Not many people came to the front door of the farm
as it was actually much easier to access the house
from the rear and through the kitchen. Whoever it
was, they were new to the area.

Katie dragged open the stubborn wooden door which

had warped over time. A man in a business suit stood there and next to him a young man dressed almost identically. This one held a clipboard.

"Good morning. Miss Reynolds," the older man said.

"Yes, can I help you?" Katie fumbled to get her arm in her jacket.

"I'm Mr. Wainwright from the Highways Agency, and this is Mr. Frankcam," he indicated the younger man who smiled and nodded a greeting. "We wondered if we might get a minute of your time?"

*

The three of them sat quietly around the kitchen table. Mr. Wainwright rearranged some papers on the table whilst the younger Mr. Frankcam toyed with his clipboard.

"It is a fantastic offer," Mr. Wainwright stated.

Katie looked blankly at the papers in front of her.

"It's a once in a lifetime opportunity," he seemed unsure about her lack of response. "It would mean you could live comfortably for the rest of your life."

Katie nodded.

"Of course, we would be demolishing both the farm and the farmhouse but this, I think you would agree, is a super offer. "

"Is it certain then?" Katie asked. "Certain that the road will run through here?"

"Actually, not through here exactly" Mr. Frankcam piped up, encouraged by a gesture from Mr. Wainwright. It felt as if they were trying to appease

Katie. "Not through the house itself. As you can see by the ecology map," he took a sheet from his clipboard. "We'll be going through the top fields, so the construction work would go at least as far as the outbuildings themselves. Of course, the farmhouse itself, situated so close to the traffic, would be essentially uninhabitable. So, logistically at least, it makes sense to clear the whole site."

"Of course," she replied.

There was a silence.

"I think what I mean is," she swallowed hard. "Does it have to happen? Do I have to accept this offer?"

"Well, that's the point of a compulsory purchase order," replied Mr. Wainwright, smugly. "It has to happen. It's been decided for the good of the infrastructure of the County. "

He folded the maps away carefully, as if this part of the negotiations had been completed.

"I must say in all of my time doing this job, I've seen various people who are sad to leave their homes but never anyone who has been disappointed with such a generous offer. I think you'd agree, it is a LOT of money."

"It is."

Mr Wainwright formally moved the papers in front of her. He took a pen from his breast pocket and removed the lid. Then he turned the pen, indicating that she should hold it. He pointed to the bottom of the papers to indicate where she should sign.

"Just here."

She looked down at the page. Turned back the pages. She had scoured many contracts in the past and knew exactly what this meant. She'd be selling the farm to the Highways Agency to build a road through the land. The land her aunt had fought so hard to preserve. She politely refused to take the pen, waving it away. She took a deep breath and gave herself some time to think. Mr Frankcam pulled a face at Mr. Wainwright. The silence in the room was palpable. Katie looked up to the corner of the kitchen to where a stubborn cobweb had eluded her best efforts at cleaning and watched as a spider worked its way across the elaborate web.

What would Aunt Liza have done?

Or her mother?

And in that moment, she steeled herself.

"If I wanted to, could I appeal against the decision?" she suddenly felt her blood rising. "Could I refuse to sell? What if I say no? There are people here relying on this farm. I need to consider them."

Frankcam interrupted her, "You could give them some of the money," he smiled at Mr. Wainwright. "I bet they wouldn't be quite so upset then."

But he had completely misjudged Katie's reaction. "Actually, I think it's time you gentlemen left," she stood slowly and defiantly. "I'll let you know my response in due course. Please, see yourselves out. "

Mr. Wainwright shook his head.

"Very well," he said, standing. "But whatever you decide to do personally with the money, the final notice will be issued by the courts on 31st May and the farm will transfer into our possession approximately two weeks after that date." And then, more authoritatively, "Your signature, as you could tell from the contract, is pretty much perfunctory, a courtesy. We would just have moved ahead more quickly with securing outside construction contracts. Compulsory purchase means just that: compulsory." He placed his pen with deliberate slowness into his breast pocket.

"We are taking the farm."

Gripping his briefcase, he followed Mr. Frankcam down the hallway. As the front door opened and Frankcam left, Wainwright turned on his heels to face Katie.

"A word of advice, Miss Reynolds. No one has ever successfully blocked a development of this nature with the Highways Agency. This project is just too big and has too much money committed to it for us to change our plans now."

Katie nodded to her adversary who strode purposely out the door.

Katie slumped into her chair and sighed. A moment later Mr. Frankcam bundled into the room mummering excuses.

"Sorry, sorry, I…" and indicated he had left his clipboard on the table.

"No problem," smiled Katie.

"You didn't see, did you?" Frankcam said, gathering it to his chest.

"See? See what?"

"The report thing. The nature study report."

"No, though that does sound interesting? What is it?
"

Frankcam visibly swelled with importance. "It's why we've never been able to buy the land before. Nature."

"Oh, nature," Katie leant forward with real interest. "What do you…"

A loud shout from the front door.

"Peter! Come along! Time to go."

And with that Peter Frankcam scurried off, giving her an apologetic smile.

What was all that about? thought Katie.

She poured herself some water and watched as Maisie and Jean lead the new rescue donkey across the yard to meet Jackson, one of the friendlier horses, tethered next to the trough. Big old Jackson, at eighteen-hands high, he looked at the new addition with genuine interest, whinnied, and then nuzzled against the donkey's neck.

The donkey seemed to recognise the welcoming signal and instantly became calm. Within moments he started eating from the trough and the two, standing side by side, one so tall and one so small made for a lovely comical contrast.

Maisie and Jean hugged one another in delight.

Chapter
thirteen

Spud, the newly named donkey, was slowly settling into the farm's daily routine, as was Katie. There was a certain calm rhythm to the days, feeding and managing the animals and sweet evenings spent mostly reading and swapping stories by the open fire. It was never particularly cold but Katie liked the way the fire played through the evening and made her feel comforted. It was the equivalent of lighting some posh candles to Hygge the evening.

Jean was even teaching Katie how to knit.

A therapist, early on in Katie's professional life, had suggested that Katie learnt a low-level distraction technique like knitting to keep her brain active while also helping her to deal with stress. Ironically, she had been too busy to learn and her first foray onto the internet to watch a How To Knit video had left her more frustrated than ever.

"In, round, out and off," reassured Jean. "That's it, in, round, out and off."

As Katie completed her first few rows she was really pleased with her efforts and held them aloft for Maisie to look at.

Maisie was less than impressed and went back to looking through the photographs in the knick knack box that Katie had allowed her to play with.

"So that's your nan and grandad then?" enquired Maisie pointing to four figures on a browning black and white photograph.

"Yes, I believe so. I never met them, though."

"That's sad," Maisie pulled a sad face.

"Yes, yes it is," reflected Katie. She carried on knitting, feeling suddenly awkward.

"And is this Liza here, with your mum?"

"That's right."

It was remarkable how alike her mother and older sister looked. The same dark colouring and long slender figures which Katie herself had inherited.

"It's a shame that they fell out. I wish I had a sister."

"Me too, Maisie, me too," Katie put her needles down and rubbed her eyes. "I don't really know why they fell out Maisie."

"It was a man," Jean stated bleakly. Katie's head

103

snapped up.

"Really?"

Had one of mum's many boyfriends come between them?

"I don't like to gossip," Jean said, though instantly seemed to regret it.

"It's fine Jean, we're all friends here. Please, tell me what you know."

Jean put down her knitting and folded her arms.

"Liza was in love with a boy from the village – and had been for years. He knew how she felt but he didn't feel the same about her. "

"Right," Katie said, willing her to go on.

"Well, your mother, who was a real beauty back then, well, she … she took a fancy to him."

"Is that right?" Katie said, unable to hide the frustration in her voice.

Maisie interjected, "Did she kiss him? Did she?"

Jean picked up her needles again.

"That's right. That's just what happened," she said, as her needles clicked into life.

Katie remembered her mother's words about Liza, being 'prudish.'

So that made complete sense. Katie's mother had bolstered her own ego by stealing Liza's one true love. Typical.

Katie went back to her needles. "Did she ever marry? Have a boyfriend? I found a wedding dress in the wardrobe."

"No. I don't know anything about that," replied Jean. "She only spoke to me about it once. Said that you're lucky to have one great love in your life. After your mother disappeared, your grandparents died pretty soon after that. Not much between them, in fact. I think it was the farm that actually saved Liza's life. She threw herself into caring for others and things that needed loving."

Katie sat quietly listening to the fire crackle as the needles clicked away.

"I vaguely remember you coming to the village for that summer," Jean said. "How old were you then?"

"I think I was about nine."

"I wasn't helping here then. There were men paid to farm and harvest and there were only a few animals here. It was a busy, prosperous farm."

"So how did you get involved?" asked Katie struggling to tame some rogue wool.

Jean lowered her voice to a whisper as Maisie went to pour herself a glass of water. "I lost my daughter, Maisie's mum, and we were suddenly all alone, the pair of us. No support, no money. Liza offered me a job here, helping out. She didn't really need me then but, well, that was the kind of woman she was."

"Jean, I'm not going to be able to save the farm, you know," Katie said. "The Highways Agency have given us ninety days and even if, by some miracle, we got a stay of execution, the rescue side of the farm runs at such a loss it is unsustainable in the long run.

105

One way or another, I will have to sell it."

Katie put her knitting to one side and reached over to touch Jean's arm.

"Jean?"

"God will find a way," Jean replied with finality. "His will be done."

And then she carried on clicking away.

Katie nodded; she had nothing else to offer. She held up her knitting to examine her progress.

The dropped stitch was obvious.

Chapter
fourteen

Katherine had finally replied to one of Oliver's
messages. It was about time for her to return his
grandma's ring. She wasn't going to make it easy for
him though. Why should she? After everything he'd
put her through.

He arrived at the farm in the second week of
November.

She instantly knew that it was him. The heavy
crunching sound of his new black Range Rover
coming down the farm track.

Ironic really. A Range Rover like his really did belong
on a farm like this instead of on the streets of South
London where he lived in his pretty Georgian town

house.

Katie went to the window and looked out at him. He got out looking simply magnificent:

White linen shirt, mid blue trousers, gold Raybans pushing back his blonde hair.

He took a moment to look round at the farm buildings, as if he couldn't quite believe what he was seeing.   It was as if he was in shock. Finally, he turned in her direction and started making his way across towards the front door.

Katie went out of the back door and around to the front of the house.

"Hello Oliver," she said dispassionately.

"Hello Katherine."

He leaned in to hug her and she gently allowed him to.

"So, this is Butterfly farm?" he wheeled around with open arms. "It's ..."

"Are you suddenly lost for words, Oliver? That's not like you."

She turned around and walked off, though she supposed he'd follow her round to the kitchen.

As they entered, she indicated for him to sit at the kitchen table and began to put the kettle on. She could tell by his grimace that he wasn't happy about sitting there.

He took a melodramatic double-take when he saw the kittens mewling in a box by the grate and leaned in to have a look at them.

"I didn't know you liked cats.""

"There's a lot you don't know about me," she indicated to him to sit back down again.

Looking uncomfortable he manoeuvred himself into position. She sat down firmly opposite him and waited. She was not going to do what she always did and help him by beginning the conversation. She found that she was very comfortable just sitting in silence.

He coughed and then began what sounded very much like a pre-prepared speech.

"I wanted to look you in the eye," he looked directly at her but then, just as quickly, looked away. "And say that I'm very sorry. I was a fool. I made a terrible mistake. "

"A mistake?" she said. "You're saying growing a baby is a mistake? No, a mistake is you losing your bank card or missing a birthday. Or even – and go with me on this - not lying to, and repeatedly cheating on, someone who thought they were going to spend the rest of their life with you."

"No, I didn't mean it like that," he said. "I mean..." he sighed. "I should have handled things … differently. I should have… spoken to you and been honest. "

Katie nodded. For a moment he seemed genuinely remorseful. "I am a child and I acted irresponsibly." She had never known him speak so openly before.

"I take it that the mother is Anna? The woman you

work with?"

"It is," he bowed his head.

"You always said she was a climber."

"I don't think I did say that."

"Anyway, good for you!" she said sarcastically. She just couldn't help herself. She desperately wanted to be the *bigger person* but it wasn't coming easily.

"So when is the baby due?"

A baby – her fiancé was having a baby. And not with her.

"December."

A Christmas baby. Katie wondered what she would be doing this Christmas.

"Will you marry her?"

He nodded solemnly, "Yes, father insisted that we make it official. He doesn't want a Hurst-Wyatt being born illegitimately."

"Wouldn't want that shame now, would we?" she said sarcastically, acutely aware that this was what had happened to her.

This was now becoming too real, too painful.

"I've come for my grandmother's ring. "

"Of course you have."

Katie walked past him and over to the mantlepiece. She removed a small China teacup and put it in the middle of the table.

Oliver raised his eyebrows in disbelief. This ring, this inheritance, this object of such high monetary value, had been sitting on the mantlepiece, in a teacup.

With a sigh, he removed the ornate black and embossed gold box and opened it.

"Checking that it's still in there?" she said, acidly.

"Don't worry. I wouldn't want that ring now. "

He seemed to realize that she was now stronger and more in charge. The power balance had tipped away from him. He bit his lip.

"Do you know, Katie. I still think we were great together. Look great together. Perhaps, when you come back to London, we could go out for a drink?"

Katie blinked hard in complete disbelief.

"Really?" she said mockingly, incredulous at this suggestion.

It was difficult to know what to say then. Everything that they had shared between them seemed to have been some kind of lie, some kind of weird dream. An utter waste of her time. She really didn't know him at all.

Molly the cat mewed at her kittens.

Maisie burst through the back door, all arms, legs and energy. She moved too close to Oliver.

"Are you a TV star?"

He pulled a puzzled face.

Katie laughed, "No Maisie, no, he's not an actor."

And then, unable to hold the thought back, "Not a paid one anyhow."

Oliver grimaced.

Jean appeared in Maisie's wake. "Maisie come on, leave Katie and her friend alone."

Then she attempted to usher Maisie out, but with little success.

"Oliver, may I introduce you to Maisie and Jean? My…" she struggled to accurately describe their relationship, "co-workers?"

Jean nodded her approval at the term.

Oliver laughed. "You mean you muck out the animals?"

Jean did not take kindly to this obvious sarcasm.

"That's right. We care for things that can't care for themselves," she flared her nostrils in disgust before looking him up and down. She had his number alright.

"Come on Maisie." she said as they left.

Maisie, having picked up on her grandmother's obvious disdain, turned and stuck her tongue out at him.

Katie couldn't believe how rude Oliver had been. Open mouthed, she now saw him for what he truly was.

"Actually, it's time you were going, Oliver," she stood and folded her arms. "Good luck with Anna and the baby."

As a parting shot she coolly said, "Oh, and Oliver?"

"Yes," he said, smiling at her.

"I'd take it as a great personal favour if you never, ever, contacted me again."

Chapter fifteen

Winter seemed to steal upon the farm. Katie had heard nothing new from the Highways Agency and was starting to hope that they might have changed their minds. There were few animals frolicking or playing now, most simply happy to make a lot of noise as they curled up in their various pens and sheds. The days had become short and Katie could feel the chill in the air. The farmhouse was cold and difficult to heat so most evenings were spent gathered around the fire. She'd become an expert at lighting it. In fact, she had become pretty proficient in most things that were of a practical nature and Jean's constant encouragement to "give it a try" meant that whilst things didn't always go perfectly, they did get done, after a fashion. Katie was physically fitter than she had been for years, her arms and legs toned from

113

weeks of digging, loading and hefting all sizes of hay. Katie had found it useful to draw up an Excel sheet for her own peace of mind and wellbeing. On it she had sheets with all of the feeds, their suppliers, costs, debts and every week she reappraised how much money the farm was losing. She was still subbing the farm from her own savings but sooner or later she was going to have to let her flat in London go. She couldn't afford rent there and outgoings for the farm as well. After all, would she even want to return to that same flat with her inheritance money? Return to that same life?

Jean, Maisie and Katie spent most December nights chatting and knitting. They were making cardigans for the Exeter Maternity Premature Unit and enjoyed talking about the babies that would wear their creations. Jean chose mainly white wool to knit with, Katie a neutral lemon but Maisie insisted on the most outlandish colours of oranges and raspberry. She used huge needles, dismissive of the fact that the larger holes weren't going to keep a new baby particularly warm. She said little babies needed to live big. She had a way of seeing life that was generous and gentle. When the hospital told them that they had too many of these types of cardigans, Jean took it upon herself to sell them to everyone she knew and that way managed to raise a few pounds for the hospital separately.

Christmas was fast approaching. The water in the

troughs had a tendency to freeze and had to be bashed most mornings to allow the animals to drink. Katie was concerned about how cold the sheds could be but Jean reassured her that it was normal for farm animals to live in sheds. The basic heating for these pushing her bank balance further into the red.

The guinea pigs hardly moved for a month; the chickens carried on with their usual day but went into roost earlier and earlier. The goats seemed angry at the fact there wasn't fresher, tastier grass to eat and the ponies, in from the fields, were in a gentle hiatus. There was a completely different rhythm now on the farm and it was tangible. Katie had only really thought of winter as skiing and Christmas parties. Now, she better understood the flow of the world, the idea that everything had a natural life cycle of its own.

She had finally written back to the conservation people, thanking them for their interest in the farm but explaining that it was going to be demolished or sold on. Either way, there was nothing happening at the top end of the farm and with the severity of the winter months she couldn't see how anything could have survived up there anyway.

"What happens at Christmas?" Katie asked Jean one evening. Jean was cleaning the brass candlesticks from the front dining room and Katie was making email enquiries to various animal sanctuaries inquiring as how they managed to get the funding they required to continue their work.

"What do you mean?" Jean asked, her hands covered in brass stains.

"Parties? Dressing up? Dinner?"

"Oh, I see what you mean," she lowered the newspaper and wire wool she'd been using. "Well.."

"Nothing," interjected Maisie. She was sitting at the table, drawing a picture of a vampire bat and colouring its fangs. "It's boring."

"No, Maisie," Jean reprimanded, "that's not strictly true. We go to church after the animals have been fed and then have dinner."

"Right and then…?" said Katie waiting for more.

"Well, that's about it. Farmers have to carry on as normal. No one else is going to sort things out for you."

"I realise that. But surely you must get up to something? Something fun?"

Katie had mistakenly assumed that families, real families, played board games together, cheated at Monopoly and fell out over charades. Things which she had never done but had always thought would be a lovely, wholesome thing to do.

"We haven't had fun since mummy died, have we Nanna?"

Jean took a deep breath, picked up her things and went through to put the candlesticks back in the front parlour.

"Nanna doesn't talk about mummy anymore," Maisie

stopped colouring, "I want to talk about her, I miss her."

She held up her picture for Katie to see.

"That's very creative," Katie said and then, more carefully. "Perhaps Nanna needs more time. Misses her so much that she needs more time. Then she'll be able to tell you about all her happy memories." This seemed to make perfect sense to Maisie who nodded in satisfaction. As Jean came back with an old clock that need fixing, Maisie jumped up and grabbed her round the waist.

"Maisie," Jean exclaimed laughing. "What's got into you?"

"Can we make some more good memories, Nanna?"

"Yes," Jean replied, looking at Katie with a certain understanding. "Yes, we can, of course we can." Katie's mind was already whirling new memories, new Christmas memories. Yes, Katie felt a plan formulating.

*

Lucy arrived at the farm on Christmas Eve laden down with a suitcase that was too big for her to carry and whose wheels weren't designed to cross the cobbles. She manhandled it into the hallway and laughed at her own ineptitude.

Katie had always been grateful for Lucy's generous friendship.

They had met on the first day of secondary school

117

when Katie - new to the area, mum with a new partner - had turned up worried and anxious. Lucy had been extremely protective of her new friend, bordering on aggressive at times and had sent clear warning signals to those who thought that it might be fun to tease the girl with the posh accent. Katie had never enjoyed change. It usually meant stress and embarrassment in equal measure. She never had the right paperwork or the right uniform and was always late, left to her own devices while her mother did shift work somewhere. Lucy had been randomly sat next to her in the hall while they waited to hear what their timetables would be.

"I'm Lucy. What's your name?"

"Katie," and she had looked away, feeling self-conscious.

Undeterred, Lucy had reached into her pocket and surreptitiously withdrawn two biscuits. She had subtly offered one to Katie who suddenly realised how hungry she was. She hadn't had any breakfast that morning. Her mum hadn't been to the shops.

Katie had taken the biscuit, devoured it and then nodded her thanks.

Lucy had smiled, surprised at how quickly Katie had eaten it. Then a fresh understanding had come into Lucy's eyes and she'd said, "I always have loads of snacks."

And then she'd offered Katie another biscuit. It was in that moment, despite Katie then going on to other

118

schools, that the two girls became lifelong friends.
All based on one girl's kindness.

Katie dragged the suitcase into the front parlour, lay it down and began to open it.

"Alright," Katie asked. "How much do I owe you?"

"No, no," cried Lucy, "this is my Christmas present to you. To say, 'thank you' for having me over for Christmas lunch."

"I can't, Lucy, I asked you to bring a few bits. At least let me pay for them."

"Katie, this is what I do for a living. These are just a few things I've accumulated over the years. Honestly it's a nothing."

Katie hugged Lucy. "Thank you. Your mum not going to miss you this Christmas?"

"If it was down to her, she'd have me living back there permanently but no, she's going to Aunty Maggie's this year, so I won't be missed."

"Didn't you fancy that then?"

"I've seen my Aunty Maggie dance on the coffee table with a glass of sherry in her hand one time too often."

"Speaking of which. Would you like a glass of something cold and fizzy before we get to work?"

"I thought you'd never ask."

*

Christmas day was wet and dark. Katie opened her curtain to see Jean had arrived as usual around six am to start feeding the animals. Jean went equipped with her wheelbarrow out into the Ark.

Katie was amazed at how quickly she'd managed to learn all the animals' names. It had helped that she had added them all to her spread sheet. Each animal had its species, name, feed type, supplier and special notes such as likes and dislikes. Katie had never thought animals could be such emotionally diverse creatures. Even the chickens which looked almost identical had their own peculiar habits; where they liked to sit and feed. And the goats! They could be the grumpiest of animals. If they didn't feed in the correct order of hierarchy they would violently try to butt heads with one other. Tina the turkey was just plain funny. She liked to have company and particularly enjoyed being with the Shetland pony, Pickles. But she also needed to be the absolute boss of the other animals and would even chase people around if she was in a mood.

Katie got up and made tea for Jean. She hadn't seen Maisie yet which might mean that the growing teenager was finally going to get a lie-in. She decided she'd leave Lucy to sleep off her bottle of prosecco. Wrapped up warmly, in woolly hat and gloves, Katie slipped on her pink wellies and took Jean's tea out to the barn. As she rounded the corner she saw Jean leaning over the wheelbarrow in an awkward position.

"Jean?" Katie stood the cup on an upturned barrel and hurried over to her.

120

Startled, Jean quickly stood up, extending a reassuring hand, "I'm fine, honestly, I'm fine."

Katie manoeuvred Jean over to a hay bale and sat her down. She looked terribly pale. The various animals watched in silent fascination at the unfolding scene.

"Jean, what is it? Do you need an ambulance."

"Of course not," she said, dismissively, though she was clearly in some discomfort. "I get the odd dizzy turn now and then, that's all. I'll be alright in a minute."

Katie sat down next to her and waited. When she seemed a little more stable, she poured away the tea before taking it over to the shed tap. She filled the cup with the ice-cold water.

As Jean sipped at it, she chided, "I'd rather have had the tea."

After some time had passed Jean's face seemed to have regained some of its colour.

"Jean. Have you seen a doctor about this?"

"Of course not. I've always been a fainter. Just have to manage it. It's only been dangerous when I've been in the bath. As a young girl I nearly drowned once. Had to unhook the plug with my big toe. Saved my life. Now I just have to listen to the signals and sit down when I feel it coming on."

"Perhaps…" Katie began.

Jean shook her head, signalling that she wouldn't accept any interference.

"Perhaps, as a grown, up I can manage my own

health concerns."

That shut Katie straight down.

"But I probably could do with a slice of toast. It's probably low blood sugar. Shall we have some?"

The two of them, their breath forming clouds in front of their faces, wandered out of the shed. The pigs were not pleased that breakfast had still not been delivered and snorted their displeasure.

"You ungrateful lot!" shouted Katie. "I'll be back out in a minute."

"Katie?"

"Yes, Jean? What is it?" Katie said, concerned.

"I forgot to wish you Happy Christmas."

She put her arms around Katie and hugged her to her.

*

After the church service at eleven am, which was absolutely packed, Katie and Lucy smartly returned to the cottage to get ready for Christmas dinner. Jean and Maisie were arriving as VIP guests for lunch at three o'clock sharp. Already the excitement was tangible although Katie was still concerned about Jean doing too much.

Both Maisie and Jean arrived at the kitchen door looking very different to normal. Jean had on a lovely tweed skirt and pussy bow blouse and Maisie had a mini skirt on and a pair of platform boots which she struggled to stand upright in.

Maisie had helped to make a trifle, which only contained a few finger sponges in the bottom because she'd been unable to stop herself from eating the rest while she'd been making it. Jean put it down on the kitchen table. She looked around the room. While there were wonderful smells from the cooking turkey and there were vegetables bubbling away on the Aga, Jean was surprised to see that the table was largely bare.

"Do you want me to lay the table?" Jean asked Lucy who stood stirring some gravy.

"No, thanks, I think we've got it all under control," said Lucy.

"Why don't you two go through?" suggested Katie.

"Through?" questioned Jean.

"Into the front parlour."

"Katie are we going to eat in that big, horrible room," squealed Maisie. "I like it in here."

Saying that, she scooped up some cream from the side of the dessert bowl and licked at it.

"Maisie!" Jean reprimanded "No fingers!"

Lucy approached Jean with a champagne glass.

"Fizz?" she offered.

"Ooh very posh," Jean seemed pleased. This was something new.

"Maisie would you like a fresh orange juice?"

"Yes please."

Katie checked on the turkey before closing the oven door. "Right, I'll put this all down low and we'll go through for our starters, shall we?"

Jean mouthed the word 'starters?' to Maisie who giggled at the thought of it.

Katie and Lucy went ahead, down the corridor and opened the parlour door. They turned to watch Jean and Maisie enter.

The room had been completely transformed. Instead of a dark, dingy space, a huge log fire glowed in the grate. The bleak overhead chandelier, instead of the normal limp bulbs, had hundreds of fairy lights draped around it and across the whole room from corner to corner. Candles occupied every space around the walls. It was beautiful and magical in equal measure. Maisie's mouth dropped open in surprise.

The main dining room table had been opened up to seat at least ten people and a pure white tablecloth lay across it. Red candles and various cut-outs of reindeer, Father Christmas and the angels adorned the table. Tinsel and Christmas crackers lay at each of the table settings.

A place holder said "VIP Jean" and "VIP Maisie." Maisie saw Jean's first. "Here Nanna, you're meant to sit here." Then she ran off, desperate to find her own. She sat down heavily on her chair and gazed around the room at the various lights and decorations.

"Katie, if I forget to tell you later, this has been the best day of my life."

The women laughed. Jean sat on her seat and

carefully examined the plate in front of her. A starter of prawns and salad was tastefully arranged on the gold and white lined plates.

Lucy started some music up on her Bluetooth speaker and Slade's "Merry Christmas Everybody!" soon filled the air. As soon as they'd finished their first course, the Christmas crackers were snapped open and Maisie scrabbled around trying to collect all the silly items which spilled out. When she discovered that the tiny pen she'd got actually worked, she was thrilled. The red paper hats sat haphazardly on their heads.

As Katie started clearing the plates away, Jean got up to help. But Katie was insistent. Jean wasn't going to be allowed to lift so much as a finger today.

Then Katie went off to the kitchen where she began to plate up the lunch. It wasn't perfect by any means; she still hadn't really mastered the art of cooking on an Aga. The potatoes were slightly too brown and the turkey, bought from the local butcher, was a little dry. Katie wasn't sure how she could bring herself to eat a relative of Tina's. It was something she was going to have to give some thought to going forward. As Katie busied herself she could hear the laughter bursting through from the front room.

Lucy was reading a joke that had come out of her cracker. Katie could just hear her and moved closer to the door to listen.

"What is the best ever Christmas present?"

There can't be a much better Christmas present than this, Katie thought, wiping her hands on a tea towel, ready to take the food through.

"No, no, I don't know," said Jean.

"A broken drum." Said Lucy.

Immediately Maisie said, "I don't get it," in a disappointed voice.

"You just can't beat it!"

And with that the laughter echoed around the house and Katie felt full of a joy she had never known before. This was going to be a Christmas to remember.

Chapter sixteen

For a January morning, it was clear and bright. Katie sauntered across the farmyard and headed to the animal sheds. The wooden door was open and Maisie and Jean were already in situ, scattering feed to the various animals that lived in the "Ark", as Jean liked to call it. There were contented feeding and nurturing sounds broken only by a cry of, "Spud, you naughty boy!" followed by laughter. Christmas had been a wonderful time, a fantastic distraction but now Katie was going to have to address the issues of the farm's debts and its long-term future.

Katie meandered out along the lane on the right-hand side of the sheds and down to the end of all the outbuildings. There were flowers, snowdrops, starting to appear and a distinctive fresh scent filled the air. She rarely came out this far, away from the animal sections, but now standing at the far end of the furthest shed she got a clear look at the immense view of the countryside which lay before her.

The land fell away beneath her across a valley that then rose up maybe two to three miles away, way beyond the top fields to the next village of Holcot. She could make out the spire of St Andrews in the distance. It was a beautiful view, restful and restorative. How would this all look in a year's time, she wondered.

A nearby bird began its distinctive call. Loud and insistent, it flew like a precision drone over a small patch of field about 50 metres over to her left.

"That's a Lapwing."

It was a man's voice.

Katie turned to see James standing alongside her, looking out over the valley. "It's a beautiful bird, and that call, it's so distinctive, isn't it?

"A Lapwing," Katie repeated to herself.

James kicked something across the floor, obviously trying to find the words. So she said it for him.

"James, I wanted to address that moment in the pub. I know it was quite a while ago but it's been playing on my mind."

She turned to look him

"I know," James said. "I know it was a mistake. I

know you're not staying."

Katie wasn't quite sure what to say to that. That moment of connection in the pub corridor had, for her, been momentous. She was completely attracted to James but how could there be any future for them? They were grownups leading totally different lives. And very soon she was going to have to leave for good.

"It wasn't a mistake."

James looked at her, puzzled. "It wasn't? Oh, actually, I think you're, well, great."

They both looked down at the floor, slightly embarrassed.

"But."

"But?" she lightly touched his arm. "The farm is going to be sold. I will have to go back to my job, the career that I've worked so hard to establish. Because, in all honesty I do miss some of it. I was good at it, really good. In fact I'm going to be picking up some of my old clients remotely now, at least until I go back."

James nodded with understanding.

"And you're happy here, aren't you?" she asked.

"I am, I understand farms, farming. I had some big plans for developing my dad's farm but it all seems like a pipe dream now. He's not a well man, you know, my father."

"No, I'm sorry I didn't know that."

"Perhaps selling the place would be the best thing,

anyway. My brother's looking to move on himself."

"Really?"

"He's looking to settle down, with Elizabeth Marshall."

Katie nodded before realising who that was.

"Is that the blonde woman I saw you with in The White Horse?"

"That's right, Emma's daughter."

"And you, have you got a girlfriend?"

"Me?"

Katie nodded and for a brief moment held her breath.

"No, not now. Was with a girl for five years but turned out she didn't want this life either."

"Oh," Katie's heart was racing.

"Met her on a sheep farm in Australia when I did a bit of travelling. She never felt settled moving back here. We're still friends though. I think she's in Bali teaching yoga at the moment."

They both stood silently.

After a short while the Lapwing started up its call again.

"Tea?" Katie asked.

"Yes, a cup of tea would be nice."

As they began the walk back, James ran his hand over the brickwork on the side of the shed.

"Is this the one you're thinking of converting into office space? It would have a lovely view over to Holcot Village if you could get some glass fitted at the far end. Probably bring in a fair penny when you come to sell it."

"Well, that was my thought as well. I did think if we could do something with this far end it could have brought in a regular income. Perhaps even enough to support the animals. If the new owners would be prepared to keep them on, that is."

"That's a big ask. Who's going to want a farmhouse, office buildings *and* a rescue centre?" he raised his shoulders in a shrug and gave a little chuckle.

Katie smiled. *He did have a point.*

They carried on walking side by side.

"I know," she said. "I tried to think of everything I could to keep the animals but it was always going to depend on who the new owners might be in any case."

"You can still hope."

"No, sadly not. Any possible options are pretty much gone now."

James stopped still and looked at her blankly.

"Meaning?"

"Meaning the Highways Agency has written to me. Given me ninety days to sign the land over or file an appeal."

James threw his head back in disbelief.

"Ninety days to find them all a new home?" he indicated the rest of the yarded areas to show the enormity of the task. Then, with resignation, he said, "I best tell my dad that it's happening, then."

"Ninety days," Katie whispered in sudden realisation of the task ahead.

A dark cloud scudded by overhead, completely obscuring the sun. But then, in a moment, it was gone.

James took hold of her by the shoulder. Then he pulled her in for an all-consuming hug.

Chapter seventeen

Lucy sat on the rocking chair watching Katie cook a shepherd's pie.

"I honestly didn't know you could cook."

"I know, who even am I? "

They giggled together as Katie awkwardly spooned the mashed potato over the dish.

"Jean has taught me so much, stuff. Woman stuff."

"Men cook too, you know."

"Oh, I know. I mean there are things that my mother never showed me how to do. Not that I blame her, she was always trying her best to be a good mother. And do you know? All those things I used to look down on…" Katie paused.

"Like what?"

"Like cleaning and making and, well, creating a home. I'm enjoying it all now. Thinking about it, I just didn't have enough time to enjoy the more peaceful, simple things in life. Work was always so full-on." She used a tea towel to open the door on the Aga.

"You've finally learnt how to use that old thing then?" asked Lucy.

"Actually, it's like driving an old car, you get used to all its more annoying characteristics." She slammed the door shut only for it to instantly spring back open again.

Lucy laughed. "Exactly."

"Lucy, I don't suppose your man would have a look at the contract I've been asked to sign?"

Katie took a pile of papers down from the pine unit and placed them on the table. Lucy moved across to have a look, moving a vaseful of early daffodils out of the way. She plonked herself down on the big carver chair and began to peruse the contracts.

"And this is it, is it? The final countdown?"

Katie nodded.

Lucy turned the pages over slowly and then took her phone from her handbag.

"I'll ask him to have a look," she said, photographing each page in turn. "I know he's an environmental lawyer but, in all honesty, I'm not sure what advice could offer. This is such a specialist field."

"Yes, I know," Katie repeated absently. And then,

with more consideration, "A specialist field. Lucy, would you like to have a proper look round the farm at a real specialist field? You've only been up this end so far, with the animals."

"Sure. It's a lovely day for it." And then, more childlike, "Can I have a go on the quad bike first?"

"You big kid!"

*

Katie and Lucy sauntered quietly around the top field and Lucy marvelled at all the different trees and bushes which dominated this part of the farm. It was much bigger than Lucy had thought and she asked some genuinely interested questions about the wildlife that occasionally skittered around them. The women avoided going too near the Baker's cattle, they were rather too big to feel completely safe around.

Katie was able to remember some of the birds' names and calls and even managed to point out the Wild Thyme and Marjoram, that she, Jean and James had sewn when she'd first arrived. It appeared to be growing well.

"But the cows don't eat that do they?" Lucy asked.

"No, no, the cows are up here to manage the gorse. "

"The what?"

"The gorse. That's the thing that provides the best habitat for the butterflies."

"But there aren't any butterflies."

"No," Katie looked around, disappointed. "And I

don't suppose there ever will be now."

"So, that's why it's called Butterfly farm? Because there used to be butterflies here."

"Apparently so. I've actually written to a chap, a conservationist. He insists that he's going to come up here and look over the whole area before its sold and see what, if anything's, been happening. You know, it's a good thing that there are people who know about this kind of thing, isn't it?"

Katie rubbed some Marjoram between her fingers and encouraged Lucy to smell it.

"Butterflies are really endangered. Environmentalists call them: the canary in the mine. It's all down to changes in the environment."

"That sounds ominous," Lucy said. "You've got to ask yourself what we're doing to the world, haven't you?"

Katie and Lucy began a leisurely stroll back towards the farmhouse. "Do you know, Katie. I think you've been given a real gift here, inheriting this place. It's given you some real insight."

"Really? It feels more like a millstone at the moment."

"I know, but in reality, what would you be doing now if you hadn't come here? "

"Working probably."

"Look at all these things you've come to understand. To do, to feel."

"Blimey, Lucy, sounds like those mindfulness classes

of yours are really starting to have an effect."

"Don't mock it, Katie. It's the future, I'm telling you. Responsible employers are going to have to make better provision for the wellbeing of their staff," Lucy said. Then she clapped her hands together. "You know, you could turn this place into a wellbeing centre"

"And do what exactly? Run 'Learn to knit' sessions?" Katie couldn't hide her frustration.

"Why not?" Lucy realised she wasn't selling her idea very well.

"Because it wouldn't make any money. The bottom line is profit, Lucy, as well you know."

They walked on thoughtfully.

"And, you've seen my knitting," Katie said.

"True."

Katie turned Lucy around at the top of the hill by the brick shed so that she could appreciate the view.

"Wow, now that is beautiful. What's that village over there? In the distance."

"That's Holcot. It would be lovely to have a house looking out over here wouldn't it? I don't think anyone could tire of that view. "

They circumvented the rest of the farm, heading for the Ark. Once inside, they picked up some carrots and wandered around feeding them to the animals. Lucy seemed charmed by the sheer simplicity of it all.

"Will you go back to work soon?" she asked, leaning on the top rung of Penelope's pig pen. She was happily burying her snout in some feed. The snorts she made suggesting her huge satisfaction with life.

"I'm going part time first," Katie said, holding out a large carrot to Spud, who bared his teeth and then, surprisingly gently, started nibbling at the top.

"I do miss the academic side of things, Lucy. I like the sword play involved when I've got a client I really believe in. I like thinking."

"But all this…" Lucy spread her arms to take in the vast number of animals that were moving quietly around their many pens. "Won't you miss this?"

Katie finished feeding Spud the carrot and then patted his neck. "Honestly, yes, but it's felt like a temporary thing all along. Like a reality TV show, "A Year on the Farm," where we all have a good laugh at how rubbish I am at dealing with animals, as well as people, and then I have to go back to my real life."

"Only, substantially richer."

"Yes. Substantially richer."

"Will you buy a house in London?"

"Makes sense to invest, I suppose."

"I'll miss visiting here. It costs me a fortune to have my meditation and yoga weekends at Sudbury Estate but I get the same sense of wellbeing here as I do there."

"Plus, prosecco."

"And shepherd's pie!" Lucy said, smiling broadly.

Katie linked their arms together and, like children, made their way back to the house.

Chapter eighteen

Katie was sitting at the table, cup of tea in hand, about to go to bed. She had fed the animals and was enjoying the peace and quiet. Jean and Maisie had gone home straight after dinner. Maisie had an interview at a local college the following day and Jean insisted that she had a good night's sleep. Katie reflected on the conversation they'd had, earlier.

"What course is it?" Katie had asked whilst washing the plates and handing them over to Maisie.

Maisie seemed confused. "What is it, Nanna, again?"

"Husbandry. Animal Husbandry," Jean had replied, wiping the table down and replacing the flowers. She'd taken the memento box that Maisie had rifled through earlier and had set it down next to the flowers. "I'll leave these here for you, Katie. You said

you wanted to know a bit more of your history."
Katie had thanked her.

"It's such a funny name don't you think?
Husbandry," Maisie had laughed. "Married to the
animals. I'm going to have a new husband."

"Can you get one for me while you're at it?" Katie
had said, handing her another plate.

*

As Katie took the lid off of the knick knack box she
realised that Maisie's course would have to be
completed elsewhere, she wouldn't be able to do
work experience here once the farm was sold. The
farm would be gone. Though, perhaps James might
be able to help out on that score.

Usually, Katie would have taken the items from the
box in an orderly fashion, one item at a time, but in a
moment of impulse she tipped the whole box onto its
side and watched as the treasures spilled out over the
table.

The charming black and white photos showed a range
of faces that were mostly unknown to her, although
there were a few there where she felt she saw some
family likeness; her grandmother, around the eyes; her
grandad's strong jaw line.

She had never known who her father had been, her
mother stating dispassionately that he just hadn't
been part of her life once she found out that she was
pregnant. She'd always insisted that Katie had only
been a few months old when the man had

subsequently died. Which was why she never really knew where her distinctive hazel eyes had come from. She'd never seen so much as a photograph of her father, a fact which disturbed her more with each passing year.

There were cinema stubs in there, as well as an old ticket to a dance held in Exeter. They seemed like memories of a bygone time when the younger Liza had been genuinely happy. Katie opened a small Valentine's card that was clearly handmade. As she picked it up, a newspaper cutting slipped out and fluttered to the floor. The card was from "Your Love Victoria" to "Darling David", her grandparents, it would seem. She felt as if she were prying and placed it back carefully in the box.

There was a lovely black and white photograph of the pair of them, along with Liza and her mother Constance standing by the back door, laughing as they held onto one other. On the back the title read, "The Family" with the date, 1971.

She bent down and picked up the cutting that had fallen to the floor. The date was a little faded but she could read it clearly enough, 3rd March 1957. The headline was "The Butterfly Farm." It detailed the plethora of blue butterflies that had been sited on Reynolds Farm and how the owner David Reynolds had decided to rename the farm because of it. He was quoted as saying that it was, "like watching a field of bluebells rise into the sky every day." And went on

141

to say that flocks of people had visited the farm to see them. He had even opened the kitchen as an onsite tearoom for refreshments.

How very entrepreneurial, thought Katie. That was my grandad.

This must have been what Liza had been trying to recreate in the top field. She'd wanted to restore the field to what it once was, in the hope of bringing back a little of the farm's history, and with it, some cash. Goodness knows they needed some. Katie was getting to the end of her savings; the part time money was still just about keeping up with her ridiculous rent in London. There was little money coming into the actual farm. A couple of charity and animal grants contributed to the upkeep of animals they had re-homed but that was about it. It was all beginning to feel a little bit desperate.

Every day she steeled herself to open and manage the bills from the utility companies and her creditors. And, while some of them had agreed repayment plans, it was clear that the farm could not carry on without a solid injection of hard cash, and soon. There was no way that Katie could keep the farm running in its present state. Her only option was to give it up, as soon as possible, like it or not. She might just be able to spin out her savings until the end of the summer if the Highways Agency weren't able to progress with their plans. This wasn't the kind of inheritance that people usually expected or

that her friends had normally received. Some had
been given huge sums of cash towards deposits on
houses or to float businesses but wasn't on the cards
as far as Katie was concerned.

She carefully replaced the mementos back into the
box. She would keep these treasures.

*

It was just after dawn that Katie heard the first
rumble. It sounded like distant thunder but, even in
her dreamy state, she still had some understanding
that thunder wasn't meant to be continuous. She sat
up slowly dropping her feet over the side of the big
bed. She had felt much more comfortable sleeping in
Liza's bedroom since she'd given it a good clear out.
Pulling her blue cardigan around her shoulders, she
moved to the window and peered out. The farmyard
looked peaceful enough although there was definitely
a rumbling coming from somewhere. She considered
for a moment that it may be one of those rare little
earthquakes that take people by surprise in England,
but quickly dismissed the idea.

She slid into her expensive slippers that had now seen
better days and moved over to the other window.
What on earth was going on? In the distance, over
the top of the farm, she could just make out
headlights of some kind.

Headlights? In the field?

It was as she was descending the galleried stairs that

the thought finally hit her. They were diggers. And
they had begun already - but without her permission.
She wrestled her coat on and grabbed her phone
before running out into the farmyard. The animals
were clearly becoming disturbed, and distressed
noises were coming from all of the sheds.

She found the number on her phone and pressed it
while managing to climb aboard quad bike.

"James? I'm sorry it's so early - you are awake, I take
it? It's me. I think they've started."

It was only then, as she was halfway up to the top
field, that Katie realised she was still wearing her
slippers. Not that it mattered.

The headlights in the distance were less ominous now
that the sun was coming up but it seemed to be
taking forever for her to get there. She was really
angry that they'd decided to go ahead with this
without seeking her permission. She hadn't signed the
contract yet and here they were ploughing up one of
her fields.

She began to calm a little as she got closer, the
diggers were still on the other side of the hedge. They
were clearly working right up to her boundary.

Then she saw the ripped-up hedgerow - her
hedgerow. A hedgerow that had been in her family
for decades. A hedgerow which she knew had birds
nesting in it.

The digger driver was using the bucket of his
machine to claw them out of the ground. A task, at

144

which, he hadn't been entirely successful.

The deep tracks of the four vehicles involved, had cut a swathe across the far field and it was devasting to look at. It was as if the earth itself had been defiled. She took her phone and began filming. She waved to the main digger operator at the front to get him to back off but he simply waved back. She made it clear that she wanted him to stop by climbing onto a section of fence and waving at him. Eventually, he got the message.

"Morning love," he said, leaning out of the cab window.

"Would you mind telling me what you're doing here?" she shouted.

He scratched his head.

"Er, digging? Gotta get it all sorted. We're building a road through here, you know."

"I know that's your intention but I think you'll find that this," she panned her phone around so that she took in the whole farm. "This is my property. And if you do anything to threaten that hedgerow or cross this boundary in any way, I will be suing you, personally."

The driver seemed taken aback if not a little confused by this turn of events. He turned off his engine. Some of the other vehicles ranked behind him, turned off their engines also. A heavy silence hung in the air.

The man got down from his digger and moved across

to where Katie was standing on the narrow fence. Funnily enough she didn't feel at all threatened, she felt strong and, what's more, righteous.

"Look love, all I've been told is to dig out the initial foundations," he removed a piece of paper from his pocket. "Here."

He indicated a map which showed the boundary of Butterfly Farm, clearly marked in red. She could see what they were hoping to do, begin the work, breach the farm, and present a fait accompli.

The sun was helping Katie think and the rushing blood sharpened her wits.

"Where's your site manager? I want to speak to your site manager, now."

The man took out his phone and spoke quietly into it. "Phil, there's a problem."

Within minutes, James had arrived and was standing next to Katie. She acknowledged him with a nod. She felt even stronger with him there, his huge presence reassuring her that she was doing the right thing.

She took in the sections of churned-up hedge which now lay, forlorn and broken on the grass. The sight of it was heart-breaking.

A 4 by 4 truck came up the field, stopped and the site manager got out.

"Morning," he said, cheerily.

"Good morning, "she was composed. "Can I have your name please?"

"Phillip Rothman. And yours?"

"I'm Katherine Reynolds, the owner of this farm and this field, right up to this boundary," she indicated the sections of fallen hedgerow.

"Ah," he nodded with fresh understanding. He waved the digger operator back. The man didn't argue. He went and stood at the back where he proceeded to light a cigarette.

Katie turned to Rothman.

"I can tell from your plans that the red line indicates the boundary between the two fields. So, I'm just checking that it's clear that you are not to breach this boundary in any way because, if you do, I will be suing for damages."

Rothman nodded thoughtfully.

"Right, ok, so this is how you're going to play it, is it?"

"Play it? Oh Mr. Rothman, you misunderstand me, I'm not playing. I have a farm that I am responsible for and as far as I'm concerned, this hedgerow and this fence is all part of it. So, you will not damage it any further. Do you understand?"

He nodded in a surly manner.

"And if I need to go to court to enforce this it will be your name on the court order."

"Do what you want, lady," he said. "It's no skin off my nose whether it's today, tomorrow or next week. But it will happen. You have my word on that."

He started walking back down the field, indicating to

147

the diggers with a rolling motion that they were going to be leaving.

The lead driver threw down his cigarette, climbed up into his cab and fired up the engine. He performed a large U-turn, churning up even more earth before heading off, taking his whole cavalcade of motorised destruction with him.

In their wake, they left a badly scarred field.

James turned his head towards Katie.

"You were magnificent," he beamed. "Even in your slippers."

He looked down and they both burst out laughing. She got down from the fence and went to see what could be salvaged of the broken hedges. While some sections seemed undamaged, having sprung back into place, there were two long sections where the hedge had been damaged beyond repair. In one of the broken sections, she saw a bird's nest. She went over to get a closer look. The tiny eggs were crushed, any chance of life lost. She let out a huge sigh at the sight of it.

Something was changed in her at that moment.

Something that she experienced at a core level.

This was wrong. It couldn't be allowed to happen again.

"They'll be back," she said. "But, next time, I'll be ready for them."

Chapter nineteen

She had decided to retreat temporarily back to London. She needed time to think.

It was good to be back in her flat, comforting and familiar. She had a bubble bath in her beautiful roll top bath using a range of elixirs which all smelled delicious. Afterwards, she lay on her bed in her lounge wear, feeling really clean for the first time in months.

It was surprising how much she had taken for granted of this world, her world.

Katie had told everyone in Devon that she had to return home to deal with some work clients but in all honesty she had needed some time away, on her own, to think things through.

Maisie took it all in her stride, wanting to know if Katie would be traveling there on a bright red, London bus but Jean had seemed suspicious of her motives. As if she knew Katie was feeling the pressure and might not even return. When the pair of them waved her off from the farm, Katie could see the uncertainty in Jean's eyes.

But would she return?

A string of thoughts flew through her mind. She could employ a manager now to help her break up the farm, sign the Highways Agency contract and then she could be done with the whole thing. After all, she hadn't asked for any of this.

She started working through the letters that her cleaner, Rosa, had left stacked at the side of the front door. Would she keep Rosa on now that she was back? Hadn't she learnt how to clean a house herself and actually enjoy it? But if she started back at work full time there wouldn't be enough time for cleaning. There was a postcard from her old friend, Angelina. She was the one who had taken up a position with a charity group working overseas. It was a picture of a beautiful lodge with a giraffe being fed from the top window. Angelina was clearly living her best life. Katie always thought Angelina should have held out for a better salaried position and, in all honesty, had always felt a little superior towards her. As if Angelina had been the one who'd been missing out.

Only now, Katie wasn't so sure.

She hurled the postcard across the room in a dismissive gesture. No, she didn't want to think about animals tonight though. And yet she knew that she had to think about them. Spud, Penelope Pig, the twiglets, they all depended on her. She couldn't just abandon them because it didn't suit her.

She had to take positive action.

So she decided that, at least for the interim, she would hire a proper farm manager. She would use the last of her savings to get somebody decent. Someone who could dispose of all the assets, rehome the livestock and prepare for the closure of the farm. She would sign the contract tomorrow. That way, she wouldn't be out of pocket for long. And, at the end of all this, she was going to come out of this a very wealthy woman. A very wealthy woman, indeed.

Her mother's name flashed up on her phone. Now was as good a time as any.

"Mummy, how are you?"

"Oh, darling, please call me Connie. 'Mummy' makes me sounds so old. "

Katie remembered the vibe of these conversations straight away.

"What can I do for you?"

"Really! Do I need to have a reason to talk to my own daughter? Is everything alright with you darling. You sound very tense."

"I'm fine, fine, great in fact. Back in London and

151

back in control again."

"Good, that's good. What did you think of it down in Devon? Isn't it awful?"

Katie didn't have the energy to tell her that, in reality, she'd had a wonderful time away, learning how to make friends, feed donkeys, knit and cook. But she quickly banished those thoughts to the back of her mind. She had to be practical now, otherwise, she'd never get anything done.

"It was ok, though, I have to admit, I'm glad to be back."

"Darling, I hope you don't mind me asking but I've heard a rumour that you and Oliver might have split up. Is that true? Are you very sad, darling?"

So this was why she had rung. Gossip. Katie lay back on the bed and let out a low sigh.

"Yes, mother, we separated before Christmas."

"But he was such a catch darling, how could you let a man like that wriggle off the line?"

Katie paused, "Connie, mother, can I ask you something personal?"

"Of course, you're my daughter."

"Have you ever been on your own? Without a man, I mean?"

"Of course I have though not for long. A single mother wasn't much of a catch in my day, but I think I more than made up for it. I had my charms, Katherine, and look how well it's turned out."

"Yes, look," Katie trying to keep the sarcasm from

her voice. But then a thought occurred to her. "Mother, do you know why the farm was called Butterfly Farm?"

"Oh, some old thing about a blue butterfly. Is that right? Liza and daddy were always going on about it when we were young. I don't remember seeing any. Not that I cared, particularly." Then, almost as an afterthought, she said, "So, the old place is sold now, is it? What are they going to do with it now? Knock it down, I suppose."

"Why mother? Why do you hate the farm so much?"

"Oh, Katherine," she seemed to soften. "It's not the farm itself, although it was a horrid, smelly place, it was what it represented. Small, parochial, not to mention patriarchal. I was the talk of the village when I left and I never really belonged there."

"The talk of the village?" Katie could hear her heart beating. "Why?"

"Why do you think? "

Katie felt a shiver run through her. On the other end of the line, she could hear voices in the background. "Mother, did my father…?"

"I must run darling, Peter has a tournament organised and I have to sort out the nets. He say he wonders how he ever managed without me. Coming Peter." And then, almost dismissively, "Love you, darling." The phone clicked off.

"Love you too," Katie whispered.

Chapter twenty

Katie sat in the window of the All Bar and waited patiently for Lucy to arrive. Late, as usual. It was amazing at how much more patient she had become over the last few months, how time had taken on a new dimension since she had taken her sabbatical; how much more she noticed about the world now that she wasn't pumped full of caffeine and adrenalin. Outside the window, people were going about their business: businessmen on mobiles, groups overloaded with shopping bags, mothers pushing prams and talking to toddlers who gazed transfixed at the colourful world around them. A young mum, much younger than Katie, stopped directly outside her window to wrestle a wet wipe from her bag in order to wipe her baby's hands. The child wriggled and complained throughout. The mother, noticing she was being watched, raised her eyebrows in mock frustration to Katie who smiled and nodded in affirmation of a job well done. The mother carried on her way. Katie wondered if the woman had envied her sitting there drinking her wine, seemingly, without a care in the world. If only she knew.

Katie played with her lunchtime glass of wine, rolling it around the glass to catch the light. It felt very indulgent to be drinking during the day, but hey, no work today.

"Katie, sorry I'm late."

Lucy tried to squeeze into the seat next to Katie, raising her small frame awkwardly up onto the stool. She balanced against the table as she finally settled herself. Katie always found Lucy's entrances amusing.

"It's fine. I'm not in any rush"

"Daniel is just at the bar, do you want anything?

"No thank you," Katie indicated her half full glass. Lucy dropped her handbag to the floor with relief.

"So, how have you been?" she enquired.

"Ok, yes, ok. Good to be back on familiar ground to be honest."

"I bet. How are Jean and Maisie? And Spud?" Lucy laughed just at the thought of Spud.

"They're fine," although in reality Katie had had little contact with them in the past few days. She found it almost painful to think about them, carrying on without her; on her farm.

"Do they know about the Highways Agency's plan to

take it all over? "

"They know its imminent, though I haven't spoken to them about how little time there is left," Katie said. "I've got a chap, Frank Brennan, a farm manager from Exeter. He's going to assess the rehoming implications for the animals. I'm speaking to him tonight about getting a plan together."

Lucy said, "You're planning on running it all down?"

"Ladies," a voice cut across them and they were joined by a very large man, balancing two coffees in his hand.

"Katie," Lucy visibly brightened. "This is Daniel, Daniel Beardsley."

Katie smiled in acknowledgement.

"And Daniel, this is my best friend, Katie."

"Hello," he said. "Are you sure I can't get you anything?"

"No, thanks, I'm fine."

He sat easily on the tall stool. He had a very gentle demeanour and for a moment Katie had to do a double take - was this the sasquatch she'd heard so much about? If it was, he had groomed his beard and hair to a tee. Perhaps Lucy had had something to do with this more metrosexual look. As he manoeuvred himself into a more comfortable position, Katie shot Lucy a wide-eyed look of approval.

After half an hour of them getting better acquainted, Katie had managed to tell Daniel a few funny stories from Lucy's school days. Finally, Lucy clambered down from her stool.

"Ok, so why don't I leave you two alone together for a while so Daniel can tell you everything he's been able to find out about the farm."

"Are you sure?" Katie said, turning to Daniel. "I'd be very grateful for a professional steer on this, Daniel." He brought up his case, flipping it open to reveal some notebooks and official looking documents.

"See you later, you two," Lucy said. "I'm really glad that you've finally met."

And with that, she kissed Katie's cheek and then - with almost childlike joy - repeated the move on Daniel. He responded with a huge grin.

"My two besties together."

As they watched Lucy leave, he said, spontaneously, "She's great."

"Isn't she?" and they both laughed as Lucy, emerged into the street, went right, realised her error and then headed off left, throwing out her hands in faux embarrassment.

"So," began Daniel. "The Reynolds family farm goes back years. Nineteenth century, in fact. And it has always been run by successful farmers."

"Right," said Katie, leaning in to look at various photocopies of old deeds.

"It looks like it's absolutely prime crop farmland but they've always farmed livestock there as well; ideal for sheep."

"So, if it wasn't for the Highways Agency do you

think it would be possible to sell the farm as a going concern?"

It would mean she'd have to settle for a much smaller pay-out but it was something she needed to know.

Daniel rubbed his chin thoughtfully, "I think it would make a great investment opportunity for the right person. Although it's run down now, it would be quite straightforward for an experienced farmer to get it up on its feet and running profitably again. It could be a real little gem. It's got all the necessary outbuildings and you have a lot of the basic assets already in place. Yes, you could do it that way if you wanted, though you'd have to be prepared to wait for a sale. There's no guarantees here."

Katie looked at the papers in front of her.

"Is this a copy of the Highways Agency order?" she asked.

"Yes, I've had someone in the office look over it…."

"I know," she said sadly. "I've spent a lot of time on it myself. It looks pretty watertight, doesn't it?"

"I'm afraid it does. As an environmental lawyer, I can tell you, from my limited experience in this field, that there are very few indicators that would prevent a compulsory order like this from going ahead. Very few."

He looked directly at Katie, "I thought with the amount of money they had offered you, you'd have been only too pleased to accept their offer."

"Yes," she said. "I thought that, too."

She looked down and touched the deeds. She realised her family had kept this farm for nearly two centuries and here she was dealing it away, in a bar in London. He waited for her to look up, to engage with him again.

"What are you thinking?"

Katie locked eyes with him. "Daniel, what would it take to fight this?"

"Fight it? As in stop the Highways Agency?"

"Yes, yes," she repeated more determinedly. "Stop them from demolishing the farm. Take the road in a completely different direction, away from the farm? Allow the farm to continue but with a new owner."

He began to mumble something, "Katie, they'd have done all of the surveys. Spent an absolute fortune."

"I know, I know, but if there is a chance, just a chance, that I can keep it together for future generations…" her voice trailed off. "Even if they're not mine. I think I have a duty, a responsibility, to at least look into it. Don't you?"

Daniel, sat back and took a deep breath, "Do you really want to know what I think? I mean, really?"

Katie nodded, though she didn't honestly know what he was going to say.

"I think, it's madness."

Katie dropped her head in defeat.

"Wait!" he put his hand across the table to her.

"Madness, to rip up such a beautiful landscape in order for us to have more cars polluting the landscape. Madness to think that this is the only way to go into our future, following the rules set down by people with big money and small ideas."

Katie was amazed.

"I think, and I hope I'm not speaking out of turn here," he said. "But, from what Lucy has told me, it seems that you have found something new and exciting here. And, she said, you seemed genuinely happy on the farm. All I can think is: what I wouldn't give to own a farm like that? Yes, you might lose a little money, but why not try and sell it to someone who'd be able to make a success of it. It'd be your legacy, in a way."

Katie angled her head, "But it would be a real fight. Take up so much time, so much money…"

"Well if the three of us can't do, I think I might know some people who could help."

"It would have to be Pro Bono work," she said. "I'd have to call in a lot of favours."

"Me too."

At that very moment Lucy appeared at the window, pulling a silly face at the two of them. It came as a blessed distraction from the seriousness of their discussion.

"I love that girl," Katie marvelled, as Lucy made her way inside.

"Me too," smiled Daniel, before realising he'd let something slip.

Katie widened her eyes in mock surprise.

As Lucy approached their table, Katie quickly turned to Daniel,

"Just something that keeps coming back to me,"

"Yes? "

"Something the Highways man said."

Daniel started to return the papers back inside his case. "Yes?" He was eagerly watching Lucy's approach.

"Something about why they haven't been able to build a road through there before. Because I think they've tried."

Daniel turned to Katie, looking bemused. "What? Do you know something?"

"Nature, something to do with nature."

And with that, Lucy was there hugging first Daniel and then Katie.

Chapter
twenty-one

Katie had enjoyed her time back in London. She had lunched with some work friends, including Gemma who brought Katie up to date with all the relevant office gossip.

"Sophia La Cruz is clearly struggling with the work."

"Really?" Katie quizzed. "Too many cases?"

"Too many and too complicated. I don't think she had the breadth of experience that Simon was expecting," she paused, looked around and then leaned in. "And, let's just say that she doesn't find Simon the most favourable of line managers."

"Meaning?"

"She hates him. Does everything she can to avoid

referring cases to him 'cos he's so aggressive. You know how he is."

"Yes, I remember," mused Katie. Her part-time work, while less exciting, had been more relaxed now she was answering to Peter Smith, another partner. He had three children under five years of age so had a bit more understanding about the stresses of normal life.

She vowed that when she went back to the office she would reach out to Sophie and offer her a professional hand, if she was willing to accept it. Woman needed to support other women if they were to have any hope of succeeding.

But that corporate lifestyle felt so far away from her current experience. And, as she pulled into Hackhurst Lane, even though she'd only been gone for 4 days, she felt herself begin to change.

Maisie ran across the farmyard, squealing with excitement.

"Katie, Katie we got some more animals. Look llamas!" and, as she pointed out into the right-hand field, Katie could make out four or five very unusual profiles.

The last thing they needed now was more animals! Where had they come from? Who has llamas!

"And three more chickens. They haven't laid yet. And I've been really busy up in the top field."

Maisie took Katie's case and wheeled it along the path to the back door. "Jean said you might not be back for a while and not to trouble you with the worry so, we adopted them all."

"Right," said Katie. "Tell me, where is Jean?"

"Mucking out."

Katie went into the kitchen and leant against the sink to gather her thoughts. What was she doing? How on earth was she going to sort out this mess? More animals to rehome.

She watched from the kitchen window as Jean appeared from the shed and stopped as soon as she recognised Katie's car in the driveway. She seemed to ready herself, shaking her shoulders slightly before heading towards the door to the kitchen.

Katie hated confrontation but she had to stop the farm growing even further.

Jean knocked gently and opened the door.

"Katie? Hello? It's me, Jean."

Katie sighed, "Come in Jean."

She sat down heavily in the large carver chair, placing her hands carefully on the tabletop. Some old flowers chose this moment to drop from their stalks.

"Before you say anything," piped up Jean, holding up a hand to silence Katie. "We had no choice, I mean, I had no choice. They were literally dying in an abandoned pen in Sussex. The RSCPA was desperate..." her voice tapered off.

Katie gently shook her head, "Jean, you know all these animals will have to be rehomed. There's no money coming in. How are we meant to feed them?

What do they even feed *on*?"

"I know, I know. But, we'll find a way, we always find a way. They're all God's creatures."

Katie shut her eyes and breathed deeply.

"Also," said Jean, tentatively. "That Mr. Carruthers, the conservation man, is coming today to have a look around the farm. "

"No, I didn't know," replied a clearly beaten down Katie. "What's the point now, anyhow?"

"Well, on the phone he said that he had to follow up on the top fields project. He has to write a report."

"A report?"

"About the butterflies."

"There are no…" Katie felt like swearing but restrained herself, "butterflies."

"I did tell him that but he said he's got to write the final findings for the conservation project."

"Ok, ok I'll deal with it," Katie said.

"I was just going to show him …"

"Jean!" Katie shouted. "I said, I will deal with it!"

Jean was hurt. She bowed her head and moved over to the back door. Immediately, Katie knew she had been mean to respond in that way.

"I'm sorry Katie, I'm not helping am I?"

And before Katie could apologise, Jean slipped out of the door and headed over to the barns.

*

After Katie had opened all the bills, she folded arms on the kitchen table and dropped her head down. She may have had a stressful job in London but it was nothing like the stress of this direct responsibility. She felt so low that she didn't even want to see the new arrivals. It would probably best if she didn't allow herself to form any new attachments.

Then she had a thought, remembered what Daniel had said. If, in some huge twist of fate, the Highways Agency didn't progress with their building work, could she sell the farm anyway? Couldn't she still get some kind of valuation about the farm's value as a going concern, with or without the animal rescue part of it?

Yes, that's what she'd do. She'd see what kind of interest there would be in someone buying the farm outright. See if anyone would be interested in owning it and running it. What about the RSPCA people themselves? Would an animal charity do it?

Frank Brennan, the Farm Manager, had been very helpful about how most of the animals could be individually rehomed, indicating who she might contact and when. She had held off from employing him full-time. Things were just too uncertain at the minute. As it was, she was starting to get overwhelmed and she hadn't been back five minutes. The doorbell rang.

At the door stood a small framed young man in his thirties. He had floppy brown hair and horn-rimmed circular glasses. He smiled a big, toothy smile.

"Ms Katherine Reynolds?"

"That's right."

He shuffled from foot to foot. "Could I possibly…I've come a long way."

She looked at him questioningly.

"Use your loo?" he added.

"Oh," she realised the conversation that they were now having. "Er, yes, of course, it's this way."

"Yes, I know, I've been here before," he said, skipping past her with some urgency. "I'm Carruthers by the way, George."

And with that, he disappeared off to the toilet.

Carruthers? Katie had expected him to be an old, fusty man. Isn't that what conservationists looked like? She really must check herself and her social stereotyping.

She closed the front door and made her way back towards the kitchen. She waited for some time and finally heard the toilet door creak open. George Carruthers stuck his head tentatively around the door.

"Thank you, so much. I really needed…"

Katie waved her hand and shook her head indicating that he didn't have to explain.

"No problem, honestly,"

George sat down at the table and began to remove sheets of paper from his briefcase. He was floundering and fussing. "Here somewhere," he murmured.

"I don't mean to seem rude, "Katie interjected. "I just wondered how long this is going to take, only.." and she pointed out towards the farmyard. She was distracted by the arrival of the llamas and was wondering who on earth might be willing to take them.

"No, no," he replied. "I just have to sign off the end of this project, your aunt was a very keen conservationist and naturalist."

"Isn't that when people get naked?" Katie amused herself with the joke. George was completely baffled at her suggestion.

"No, no. She loved plants, the environment and such."

"Ah." Katie realised her joke hadn't hit home and felt a little deflated. "What do you need from me?"

"Just a few words about what you have done to manage the fields and what the effect has been on the butterfly situation."

Katie nodded her head in agreement. This wouldn't take long then.

"We kept the Hereford cows as was previously suggested."

"By me," he said, sounding just a little smug.

"By you?" she acknowledged his project management with a nod. He seemed very pleased with himself. She continued, "We cut back and restored the Marjoram and Wild Thyme growth by the hedge row. It took all day. Actually, Maisie said she's been busy in the top field while I've been away but I haven't had a chance to see what she's done yet."

He nodded vigorously, noting it all down on part of the report. "And?" he quizzed.

"And," she paused. "'And' nothing. We haven't seen any butterflies. None at all."

"Ah," he wrote her response down. "What about ants?"

"Sorry?"

"Ants? Have you noticed any increase in ants, types of ants, behaviours?"

Katie laughed, "Mr. Carruthers, I don't know anything about butterflies let alone ants, or their behaviours. Is that really of importance here?"

He suddenly seemed to take his role very seriously, pulling back his shoulders before he said, "Ms. Reynolds!" Katie wrinkled her nose at his officiousness, and he duly softened his tone.

"Katherine? Katie," she smiled appreciatively, prompting him to continue. "The whole natural life cycle depends on the total environment and that starts with things like the plants and the ants. We even bought some caterpillars in from Sweden last year though with disappointing results. The caterpillars trick the ants into taking them into their nests over the winter."

"Sweden? Right," Katie's estimation of Mr Carruthers was rising by the minute. He was so keen and there was something truly infectious about meeting someone with such a passionate for their work. All the while, he was scribbling furiously.

"So, is that it?" she asked. "Are you done?"

He pushed a form across for her to sign.

"Yep, that's it I'm afraid. Just sign here please," and he indicated a space for her signature.

"How often are you successful with this stuff?"

"Butterflies? Not so much, really. In fact, the Big Blue has only been bred successfully in very carefully controlled, almost laboratory-like conditions," he sighed, disappointed. "But we have to keep trying. We owe it to future generations to keep carrying on."

Suddenly, there was a huge commotion out in the farmyard. Metal clanged and there were shouts and banging. The back door swung open and Jean entered in an excited state with muck across her face and jumper.

"Katie, the llamas have got out and got into the Bakers'."

Katie turned urgently to George, "If that's all, I've got to…" and she pointed to the door as she rose to her feet.

"Of course, if I could just take a few final samples from the top field?"

"Yes, yes, but you'll have to take yourself up there."

"Thank you," he shouted after her, as she ran headlong through the door following Jean.

"No, problem," she shouted, without looking back.

And with that, he gathered all his papers together, checked on the plastic containers in his rucksack and readied himself to trudge up to the top field.

Chapter
twenty-two

James was striding purposefully through the farmyard with two sheepdogs, trying to herd the llamas back to their field. Jean was fussing, waving her arms in a forward manner and Maisie was laughing wholeheartedly at the unfolding scene. One llama decided to try and jump a hedge instead of going further up the lane to enter via the gate. But the hedge was too dense and, rather than try again, the llama decided he'd be better off following the others. Katie, once again out of her depth, started making an odd "Shooing" sound in order to give the impression that she was, in some small way, actually helping. Though her efforts felt pathetic even to her.

The dogs seemed ridiculously well trained and James had them moving by inches to cut off possible escape routes. She watched them operate in awe, and was hugely impressed by how quickly they responded to each whistle and utterance that James made. He looked magnificent as he took charge of the whole debacle staying minutely focussed on the job at hand. By the time the big, shambling llama had moved through into the field, Jean was there to swing the gate shut. And suddenly, their little game was all over. Now that they were safe, Katie realised how much fun they'd had rounding them all up. There was also a huge sense of relief.

"Thank you, James."

"It's fine," he said. "They pushed through the narrow hedgerow at the bottom. I'll put a temporary gate across it, to make sure they can't do it again."

He turned to go.

"Would you like a cup of tea?" she asked, tentatively. He looked at her squarely and took a little time to reply.

"Let me get a gate up first," he said. "We don't want a rerun of this again, do we?"

"No, right. I'll get the kettle on." Katie was suddenly excited. She turned to Jean. "Tea?"

Jean looked exhausted, "No, I'll get off and clear all this muck off me." She looked down at her hands which were covered in mud.

James strode away to set about to his work.

"Jean," Katie moved close to her. "I'm sorry Jean, really."

"Don't be silly, for what?"

"For being angry earlier. For not being a better person. For not seeing that you were only trying to help."

Jean smiled at her. "Liza told me you'd be just what this farm needs right now. And she was right."

What we really need, thought Katie, was a huge injection of cash along with a big dollop of divine intervention.

*

A warm, wholesome sun was beginning to set. Midges darted in and out of the shafts of light that fell across the yard. Maisie, who had been, rather annoyingly, learning how to whistle, stored the buckets of feed by the side of the metal shed before returning the canvas bags back to the storage area. Katie looked out over the pink tinged yard and, amused at Maisie's terrible rendition of "Shape of You," waited with a mixture of excitement and nervousness for James to return for his cup of tea. The farm was settling for the night. A truly peaceful time.

Katie's phone rang. She didn't want to answer it. She was happily living here now, in the moment. Being a grownup was draining. Lucy's name flashed up. Katie answered.

"Lucy?"

"Katie, hi, me darling. Thought you might want to know, Daniel has filed a court order to temporarily stop the Highways Agency pressing ahead with the work, though it's unlikely to be granted, he says. Looks like our case isn't strong enough. He says he can't go the "heritage and greenfield sites" route that we first thought. It's not in court until next Thursday though, so nobody should be digging until then. I thought you should know."

Katie felt winded. "Right, I thought it was kind of a long shot but…"

"Don't give up Katie. Don't give up yet! We might still find something to stop them."

Katie moved over to the mantel piece and touched the old newspaper photograph that she had found in the cardboard box. Jean had found a simple frame for it and it stood looking out over the kitchen.

"Lucy, we've got to be realistic, it's like David and Goliath."

"Exactly, and look how that turned out."

Katie sighed, resignedly, "Lucy, I'm not strong enough for this. I just haven't got the energy. I'm making it all up as I go along."

"That's life, Katie. We are all winging it, every day." The call ended and Katie looked at the faces of the relatives that she had never known. They seemed to stare back at her. Suddenly there were footsteps in the hall.

"Katie?" James stood in the doorway. "Are you ok?"

"I don't know," she replied. "I really don't know."

Over tea from thin, China cups Katie related the
stories of London up until the arrival of the llamas.
James pulled sympathetic faces at each turn and
seemed genuinely interested in what she had to say.
"So, will you keep them?" he asked
"Of course not, "Katie flashed back. "What do I
know about keeping llamas?"
James nodded deliberately.
"As much as any farmer who tries a new stock."
He watched as Katie removed an old tea cosy from
the pot and poured a dark brown tea. Everything she
did now seemed so old-fashioned, traditional yet
wholesome.
"You know Katie, you don't have to be good at
everything - to enjoy it, I mean."
"What do you mean?"
"Well," he looked at his cup as he carefully
considered his response. "It seems to me that you
have spent a long time getting to be great at some
things," he paused, reaching for an example. "Like
lawyering," he looked to her for reassurance.
"Right," she said, sipping her tea.
"But you can still pursue something, just for the sake
of it, you know. Just for the pleasure of it, without
having to be 'the best' at it. Or even good at it."
For a moment Katie wasn't sure if she was being
criticised or not. She had never allowed anyone to
see her real self and this all felt very new and very

scary. Was he right? Had her defence systems which, for years she'd thought had been keeping her safe, actually been working to keep her isolated and lonely? "But I like being good at things," she wriggled in her seat. "And, that's easy for you to say when you don't have to think about where the next penny's coming from."

She was in defensive mode and felt she had won her point.

He smiled at her. "You think I don't have my own worries?"

"Your dad owns the house you live in, doesn't he? "

"He does. Your point?"

"So," she said, suddenly feeling uncomfortable and out of her depth. "He wouldn't throw you out, would he? You've got family."

"Katie, I don't think you understand. My father's got Parkinson's."

"I'm so sorry…I…" she reached forwards in genuine apology.

"It's fine, you didn't know. You were just teasing me."

But she felt the mood between them change, become more brittle.

"He can't manage the farm anymore and, in all honesty, we brothers are probably going to have to sell anyway when the highways agency step in here. We're going to need a suitable care home for him when the time's right and the farm will have to be sold. It's going to lose so much money we might as well cut and run."

"Run?"

He placed the cup firmly down on its saucer.

"I've already secured a place on a tied farm in Kent. A cider orchard, would you believe?"

No. She couldn't believe it.

"Tied?"

"It's where you get a place to live and part of the profits, all tied to the job."

"Ah," she said, unable to keep the tremor out of her voice. "When will you have to go?"

"September, probably. Enough time to work out what's happening here then sell up and sort out my dad."

They sat quietly. In the distance they could hear Maisie half whistling, half singing, "I'm every woman."

Could things actually get any worse?

Chapter twenty-three

The following Thursday, at noon, Katie heard the diggers arriving at the top of the farm. The whump, whump noises and the smell of burning gas in the air alerted her immediately.

"That's it then," Jean said forlornly throwing a bucket of clean water across the yard floor. She picked up her broom and began to vigorously sweep the detritus away. "It's begun."

Katie ran to the kitchen and picked up a voicemail from Daniel.

"Hi Katie, its Daniel. Sad to say that we didn't get a further stay on the development," he sighed. "I am really sorry. The judge was actually very sympathetic and acknowledged all of our arguments but came down on the side of Highways Agency. Said that so much money has been invested already and that although the knock-on implications for the rural community were huge she couldn't hold up progress for a purely ethical argument. She's given you two weeks to sign and complete. They'll be enforcing it regardless then and the transfer of monies will just be more complicated.

"She went over the rest of the stuff: findings, reports, blah, blah, blah but said she would look at an appeal if we made one." He paused and then went on quietly, "I did my best, Katie, I really did."

"Anyhow, if you want to talk it over, think about appealing … well, hopefully, I'll speak to you tonight. Sorry."

*

Katie, Jean and Maisie stood at the top hedge, at least what was left of it. Looking across the field, the three of them felt like the only survivors of some vast military action.

The diggers powered down and the distinctive figure of Mr. Rothman approached them from the opposite side.

"Afternoon ladies," he smirked, before making a mock bow. "So, you've heard the court's decision, I take it?"

The three were unresponsive. "Well, I'll be getting on

179

with the job at hand then. Getting through this mess."

He indicated the scarred trenches that were ranged around him.

Katie said, "I think you'll find, Mr. Rothman, that I still have two weeks to sign over the farm."

He threw his hands out in frustration, "And then what? More delaying tactics?" He pointed at Katie, "You've finally run out of road Ms. Reynolds!"

One of the workers, who'd been knocking in thin metal rods, laughed uproariously at this. "Run out of road! Ha ha! That's a good one boss."

Mr. Rothman, suddenly realising what he'd said, laughed at his own joke. He turned towards some of the other workers to explain what he'd just said but, in the process, slipped and landed awkwardly on his elbow before falling into one of the low trenches.

It was all Katie could do not to laugh.

To her credit, Maisie didn't laugh. She slipped through a gap in the hedge and went over to help Rothman clamber out. She grabbed his elbow in a bid to help him, only for Rothman to pull his arm away. He shot a look at the workers, daring them to say anything. Then, having scrambled out, he stood on the side of the trench attempting to wipe the mud from his knees.

"What's that?" Maisie asked, pointing down into the hole. "Look, there!"

The other two women passed through the hedge

before going over to join her. There was something knobbly sticking out from the bottom of the open trench but they couldn't quite make it out.

"It's a dead body!" Maisie cried, and, when they looked at it again, they saw that it did indeed look like a curved piece of bone.

A number of the workers surged forward to take a look. There were other shapes protruding from the wall of the trench which indicated that there might be more bones down there.

"Animal bones!" Rothman said, dismissively.

"Not so fast Mr. Rothman," Jean said. "I think you'll find that during the great plague, the folk round here buried the dead on the outskirts of the villages to prevent further infection."

Katie felt Jean was working on a plan here and was in no mood to stop her.

"I heard that, too," she said.

"And if we're right," Jean continued. "You're going to have to give them the proper respect they deserve. You won't be able to dig any further."

Rothman took stock. "Missus, them there are animal bones. Anyhow, I've dug up whole graveyards before. We have procedures for this kind of thing and, let me tell you, even a few dead villagers aren't going to stop this road going through."

He turned and ushered his men away, though they were clearly enthralled by this new discovery.

*

Long after the men had gone, Katie said to Jean.

"Is that true?"

The three of them stood looking down at the odd shapes in the bottom of the trench.

"No, of course not," Jean had a twinkle in her eye. "That's obviously a cow bone. Any true country folk could tell you that but by the time they work that out with all their tests, we'll have grabbed a few more weeks to find homes for our lovelies."

"Ah, very clever."

Maisie hugged Jean tightly. "So clever, Nanna."

Chapter twenty-four

Katie was wandering down the High Street when she caught sight of the iced buns in the window of Emma's Tea Room. These were the ice buns which were famous throughout the county. Jean had said that Emma would take the recipe to her grave rather than disclose it to others. This was a traditional recipe, she insisted, and therefore sacrosanct. Only family members knew the real secret of how to make them.

Family. Katie had been so busy at the farm that she hadn't had a chance to really follow up her own historical family connections in the area. The wedding dress that hung in the wardrobe would need to be dealt with, disposed of, perhaps? And that had got her thinking. Might Liza have actually been married once?

Katie hadn't wanted to ask Jean any more directly, it felt too intrusive to be probing her about something that possibly wasn't common knowledge. After all, Jean hadn't offered any information on it, even if she did know.

But Katie was keen to find out more about her past and had decided to start researching her own family history.

Jean had suggested that she start at the local church where there were bound to be old records of her family down through the generations. She spent the morning phoning around possible sites where she might be able to send some of the animals to, managing in the process to rehome two bantam hens and a family of guinea pigs. After that she decided to take herself off for some peace and quiet.

"Morning," said an older gentleman who was tending to some wilting daffodils in the church yard. "Can I help you?" As he stood she realised it was Frank Stokes who looked after all of the community buildings.

"Good morning, Mr. Stokes," Katie replied. "Is the church open, do you know?" She pointed to the arched doorway.

"Aye," he replied. "I always keep it open for visitors when I'm on the grounds. "He stood upright in a slow and awkward fashion. "Ooh, me back. Katherine, I'm getting too old for this."

"No, you're not," Katie reassured him. "May I?" She indicated the entrance.

"Yes, my dear, go in and have a look. I'll be here if you need anything.

Although she had attended a service there on Christmas day, she hadn't really paid any attention to the building itself.

The arched entrance contained numerous noticeboards welcoming visitors and members of the community. A playgroup met each Tuesday and Thursday and a slimming club also advertised its services. Somebody had defaced it by drawing a huge bottom on one of the silhouetted figures adding the words, "Body positivity." Notes to bell ringers and leaflets for community support littered the two stone benches either side of the entrance.

To get into the main body of the church she had to wrestle with the brass handle on the huge oak interior door. At first, she thought she was doing something wrong until she realised you had to lift and twist to get the door to swing open. The first thing she noticed wasn't the arched ceiling or many sculptures on display but the sheer amount of light that swept in from the stained-glass window behind the altar. It wasn't a particularly big church but it had, for the three hundred plus years that it had been standing, watched generations of families come and go.

How many people would be using it once the Highways Agency moved into the area? Would it ever be used properly again?

Crests from both world wars lined the walls with the names of young men recognised for their bravery. She read some of their names and for a moment gave thanks for her own happy life. She really must keep her own troubles in perspective, she thought on reflection.

She made her way around, studying the various paintings and sculptures on the outer aisles and, coming across the far end of the left aisle, ran her hand along the huge marble christening font. How many crying babies had that seen in its years of service? She couldn't help smiling at the thought of it. The font itself was a thing of beauty.

She sat on a front pew and gazed at the beautiful stained-glass window, the colours playing across the white altar cloth. So peaceful. She had never been religious herself. Her mother had never really gone to church and, moving from place to place, Katie had never been part of any settled community. She wondered what it might have been like to be welcomed somewhere, into a group. It would be nice to be part of something where, if you left, you might be missed.

After a few minutes of this, she carried on around the church to a small chapel that contained the large alabaster tomb of a knight. She read a little about his life and his support for the king before deciding that she'd have to find out more about him when she got home.

Home. Where was that?

In a small room off from the nave of the church lay numerous leather-bound books. Clearly, with dates displayed on the covers, these were records of births, marriages and deaths. Would she find herself in here, she wondered?

They were all weighty tombs. Just opening the front cover of one took a greater effort than she'd expected.

The one she was looking at was a very old book. The handwriting, in faded ink, was indecipherable even if she had wanted to analyse something. The first date she could make out was 1723. A church with real history!

As she made her way round to the newer volumes, she began to get some idea of just how many people must have devoted themselves to the upkeep of a church such as this. Something timeless was here, something that transcended the lives of the villagers themselves. That added up to a whole community stretching through time.

"Are you looking for something?" a man's voice interrupted her meditations and she immediately thought she was in trouble, in a room that she shouldn't be in.

"No, No," Katie said, gently closing the book she was

looking at. She looked at the man standing in front of her.

He offered her his hand.

"Hugh Phillips" he said. "Interim vicar of St Stephens and St Botolph's." His hand felt cold.

"Hello, I'm Katie Reynolds, Liza's niece."

"Ah, I've heard all about you. Up at Butterfly Farm? Yes?"

"That's right."

"I hear it's all going ahead with the sale now, is that right?"

"I'm afraid so," Katie had to take a breath in order to explain. "I'm just trying to find homes for the last of the animals. Before they start to demolish it."

The vicar turned to go but then stopped himself.

"That is such a shame. Liza was a wonderful human being and did her absolute best for everyone in her care," he extended an arm to lead Katie back into the main body of the church. "Shall we?"

Katie did as he suggested, though she wasn't quite sure where they were headed.

He continued, "The thing with Liza is that she was a very private person. She kept all her battles to herself, even the cancer. Nobody had any idea that she'd been fighting off the Highways Agency for all those years. I believe she thought she had succeeded too."

"What makes you say that?"

"Oh," he moved over to the font. "She told me once

at the annual church fayre. I didn't understand it fully but something she kept talking about nature."

"Nature?" Katie asked.

Where has she heard that before?

"Yes, I'm sure that was it. Something about a conservation project and nature. I'm sorry, I'm not making any sense."

Ah, Katie thought, the Blue Butterfly project. She shook her head, regretfully.

"Unfortunately, that didn't work out. No butterflies I'm afraid. "

"Pity," he said. Then he gestured to the font, "Isn't it beautiful?"

"It is. Very much so," she looked again at the eight sculptured sides, decorated with fruit and cherubic angels playing. The vicar began stacking some of the hymn books.

"And to think you were christened here, just a tiny baby."

"Sorry?" Katie was dumbstruck.

"Yes," he turned back to her, registering her surprise. "You didn't know?"

"No," she couldn't quite take it in. A part of her history that she simply had no knowledge of.

"Goodness, I had no idea. My mother never told me." She was trying to process the information. "Is there anything else in here about my family?"

He pointed to one of the plaques on the wall nearby. It read: Herein Lies the body of Thomas Reynolds

Son of Frederick Reynolds 1743-1787 A Good man of our Parish. Not only did Katie suddenly have family, but it also seemed that they went back an awfully long way in this village.

"Wow, "she said. "This is all new to me."

She had a thought then: what about her father? Had her father lived here, in this self-same village?

"I'm sorry to ask," she said. "But might there be a list somewhere of the people who attended my christening?"

He went to go back to the annexe.

"I'm afraid not," but then, over his shoulder. "But you could always ask Mrs. Marshall."

"Mrs. Marshall?"

"Yes, Mrs. Marshall. I'm sure she would be able to help."

This drew a blank with Katie.

"Who's Mrs. Marshall?"

"Mrs. Marshall. Emma. The lady who runs the tearoom."

"Why would she know?"

The vicar looked at her quizzically.

"Well, because she's your godmother."

Chapter twenty-five

The next few days fell into a busy mess of phoning up animal shelters and begging them to take some of the animals. Katie found everyone she spoke to was really kind and really wanted to help but tended to give her other phone numbers to ring. She managed to get someone to take three of the goats but couldn't rehome Gruff with anyone; too old, too aggressive and set in his ways.

She watched Jean and Maisie from the window and could see they had lost the spring in their step. The lack of energy around the farm was tangible. Maisie even said that the last of the hens were refusing to lay.

"They're upset," she said.

"How can they know?" Katie said, trying to reassure

her.

"Oh, they know alright," Maisie confirmed. "Cleverer than us humans these animals. They're missing their friends."

Later that day, Jean entered the kitchen. "The second barn," she said.

"What about it?" replied Katie, frantically trying to get through to the electricity company who were now threatening legal action.

"The roof's gone."

"Gone?" Katie looked quizzical.

"Gone, leaking, bad."

"Right. Thanks for that clear analysis."

An automatic voice came through on the phone requesting the caller to hold.

"Worth repairing, Jean?"

Jean shook her head. The women looked at each other. They knew it was over.

Katie lowered the phone. "Jean, I…"

An automatic voice distantly repeated the same instructions to hold.

Jean's eyes brimmed with tears, "I'll move Spud and the pigs."

And with that she turned to leave.

Within a beat a voice chirped up, "Hello, sorry for keeping you waiting, my name's Isra. How can I help you today?"

And for a moment Katie didn't know where to begin.

"Katie, Its me."

"Lucy, give me some good news, please! It's been a nightmare here."

"Oh you poor thing. Well, the important stuff."

"Yes?"

"He told me he loves me."

Katie realised that other people's worlds weren't as troubled as hers and held so much joy and possibility.

"Daniel?"

"Yes, of course Daniel!" Lucy sounded thrilled and triumphant that he now appeared to be staying the course.

Katie hadn't even thought about her own love life. James came over often, fixing and helping out but nothing more and Oliver hadn't messaged her since she'd stood her ground.

"I'm glad. He's a keeper."

"Yes, I think he is. You?"

Carrying on her conversation, Katie started up the stairs for bed with a tiny puppy wrapped up under her right arm. Daisy, the sheepdog, had given birth to six beautiful sheepdog-mix puppies but this one was too small. She immediately named him Acorn. He wasn't feeding and Jean had told Katie she would have to try bottle feeding him through the night. In all honesty, she didn't know what she was doing. It felt wrong taking him from his mother, but she knew he definitely wouldn't survive if something wasn't done. He hadn't learnt to suckle. Things had got a lot more real and genuinely important in this new world. Life and death were happening all around her. "No romance to report I'm afraid, I wouldn't have the time, anyway. Look, Lucy, can you do me a favour? "

"If I can?"

"Can you stop off at my flat and check everything's ok?"

"In London? Of course. You coming back any time soon?"

Katie lay Acorn next to her pillow on a warmed blanket arranged so as to fully support him. She sat next to him, covering his tiny body with the sleeve of one of her cashmere jumpers. "I'll be back this month. I'm applying for permanent part time at work. I've been done quite well working from home. Until now."

"When you say, 'working from home?'" Lucy pressed.

Katie knew exactly what she was getting at.

"Yes, from home, from here. Butterfly Farm," Katie realised where her home actually was. As temporary as that might be.

As she cuddled up next to Acorn and looked at the numerous bottles of formula she'd prepared to get him through the night, she wondered what the next day would bring.

Chapter
twenty-six

Getting through the night was tough. Acorn had
struggled to feed on the formula the vet had left,
though, on the upside, he had survived the night. In
the small hours, Katie wondered how parents did this
with real children, real babies? As it was, she was
checking him every half hour and at one stage fetched
a hot water bottle to put under his blankets. Thinking
about others, caring about something other than
herself, had provided Katie with a steep emotional
learning curve, although, in all honesty, she was
enjoying it. She was starting to realise just how
selfish and privileged she had been living in London

and how lonely that had made her.

As Katie carried Acorn back out to the wooden shed to spend some time with his mother, she noticed Jean leading Spud out of the barn.

"Jean?"

"Morning. How's the little one?" she indicated that Katie was still in her pyjamas even though she was wearing her pink wellingtons. "Rough night?"

"Can you tell?" Katie smiled before holding up Acorn. "Just give me a minute and I'll pop him back with Daisy."

In the barn, Katie could hear little whelps and sniffles coming from Daisy's bedding area. Daisy was in the process of suckling her other babies and it was a beautiful sight to see. She offered Acorn to Daisy's nose and, straight away, Daisy licked him and fussed him. Acorn immediately roused himself at her touch. Katie placed him down next to his brother and four sisters and he was immediately lost in a mass of warm bodies.

Katie breathed a long sigh of relief as she straightened, pulled a hairband from her wrist and set about securing her long curly hair in a high ponytail. Then, she froze as something remarkable happened. Acorn began to push himself forward in spite of the others. When he was close enough, he nuzzled his mother's teat and, suddenly realising what he should be doing, he latched on and started feeding. Within minutes, he was feeding properly.

Overwhelmed with tiredness and relief, Katie left the shed in order to tell Jean the good news. For once, something had gone right.

Jean was outside, giving directions to someone who was reversing their horsebox back into the yard.

"Jean?"

Jean gestured for her to come forward. Then, as the driver parked and got out, Jean moved to turned to introduce the pair of them. The new arrival was, a short, kindly faced woman wearing a bright red headscarf.

"Katie, this is Penny Woolston. She's taking Spud."

Katie's head snapped backwards, "What do you mean, she's taking Spud?"

Jean seemed embarrassed by Katie's response.

"Taking him. She's going to try and rehoming him for us."

"But what about Jackson? We can't separate Spud and Jackson. And where is he going, exactly?"

Penny turned and nodded to Jean, indicating that she would give them some space. She made her way over to the back of the horse box.

Conspiratorially, Jean took Katie to one side. "You see, I've done my best to get Spud settled, but there's no way she can take a horse like Jackson as well. "

Katie looked squarely at Jean knowing she was right. These things had to be done. She just hadn't expected things to end so quickly. The animals had to go, there was nothing else for it. Jean and Maisie

197

would move on with their lives, the farm would be demolished and the village would be forever changed. Katie steadied herself, nodded and turned to go out towards Jackson's field. She didn't look back as she heard Spud's hooves clattering across the cobbles. As she got to the gate, she could see Jackson cantering backwards and forwards frantically. In the distance Spud's loud heehawing slowly faded as the horsebox was drawn down Hackhurst Lane

*

Katie spent most of the afternoon looking at some legal documents that the office had sent through to her. She had written to HR about the possibility of continuing to work part time from home and was waiting to see what Simon Martindale had to say. She was so senior now that her skill set was always in demand. She had not even bothered to open all the emails she'd received from the various recruiters, alerting her to high powered vacancies in other, top tier firms. Of course, they would get a fat fee if they could place someone like her, so she couldn't blame them for trying.

Even with a lot still to do at the farm, the change in her mindset was becoming clearer. She didn't want to spend her entire chained to the office although she did miss the academic rigor and the challenge that came with working in a big legal practice. She hoped that part time work would be able to reconcile those two sides to her.

The money from the Highways Agency would no doubt cushion her from any financial hardship she might face in the future. That meant she could pretty much do as she pleased work wise. So why did it suddenly all feel so very empty?

She rubbed her eyes and looked at the shrinking list of animals which still needed to be rehomed. Jackson, Gruff, eight hens, Penelope Pig and Tina the turkey. Tina wasn't going to be easy to place. Where do you put a Turkey that thinks she's the boss.

Katie's phone rang.

"Ms. Reynolds?" she instantly recognised the voice of Mr. Rothman, the odious construction supervisor. "Good morning."

He gave a spluttering cough before continuing. "I wanted you to know that the bones we found were, as I thought right from the start, animal bones. And, in light of the recent delays, we will be resuming work at the farm within the week."

He paused to let that sink in. "You don't get it, do you Ms. Reynolds. This area needs better infrastructure and I'm sorry to say but the needs of the many outweigh the needs of the few."

"Let me stop you there," she declared. "Firstly, don't tell me you're sorry because you're not and, secondly, whilst I would usually agree with your sentiments about 'the many', I have seen the alternative structural plans for this road. You could have easily taken the road three miles to the North and, in so doing, avoided numerous small holdings on the way. Could you not, Mr Rothman?"

"Well, yes that is true but…"

"That's not about the few though, is it Mr. Rothman? That's about money, pure and simple. It's cheaper to buy me out, rather than spend more having to cut through the sedentary rock further north. True?"

She waited, breathing heavily from her outburst.

"Yes, but…"

"But, whilst I get the money, history tells us that the villages in the immediate vicinity suffer dreadfully. Prices for land falls, farms go out of business, people desert once vibrant small communities." She paused for a moment, "So don't come at me claiming the moral high ground."

"Ms. Reynolds," he seemed to be enjoying her tirade. "You, my dear, are missing the bigger picture."

"Let me just get this straight. By focussing on the bigger picture I can. My understanding is that you cannot cross my land until the money is cleared by the bank. Is that correct?"

"Ms. Reynolds," he slowed to a patronising drawl. "I have spoken to all of my superiors and you'll find that the money is being deposited this week and will be cleared by Saturday."

She paused, she had nothing left.

"No more delaying, no more games," he laughed. Then, with a mocking laugh, he said, "I think you'll find that in terms of chess, that's pretty much check mate."

And with that he hung up.

Katie threw her phone across the table in frustration.

Chapter
twenty-seven

Katie liked being organised. She liked to write things down on a list before ticking the items off one by one. While she was adept at Excel sheets, and pretty much all things technological, she felt a real sense of calm whilst writing out her to-do lists.

Her beautiful journal was designed with positive affirmations on every page. Her mother had thoughtfully sent it to her on her birthday. She had enjoyed filling it with her thoughts, goals and her various lists. But she also kept it very private. To read through the challenges of her life, explicitly stated, soothed her. Made her feel a little more in control.

Katie was aware of Maisie watching her as she worked through her lists, crossing out certain items while amending others. There was a lot of work still to be done before the farm could be shut down completely. And she found that every couple of minutes she came across something else that needed to be done.

Cutting off utilities. Clearing the house. Notifying the post office. Goodness, moving flats was hard enough, clearing a farm before it could be levelled was a nightmare.

"Being an adult is hard, isn't it Katie?"

Katie put her pen down and looked across at Maisie with a cup of tea in one hand and a chocolate biscuit in the other.

"It can be. It can be," Katie said, feeling the need to lift the mood. "There are a lot of good things about being an adult, too. "

"Like?"

"Like, how many more nice people are out there than you think. All those local farmers that have offered you work experience for your course."

Maisie pulled a pained face.

"Like…" Katie struggled to find another answer.

"Like not having people telling you what to do all the time."

"But the roads people are telling us what to do, aren't they?"

Katie couldn't argue with that logic.

"Well, yes," she tipped her head sideways. "But we all have to live within the rules whether we like it or not."

"But you do like living here, don't you?" she looked thoughtfully at her biscuit. "With us?"

"Of course," Katie moved around the table and pulled Maisie tight against her. "I love you, Maisie." At that moment, Jean walked through into the kitchen

The thoughts fell out of Maisie unchecked, "Then you mustn't go. You must stay here and live with us. You could be a farmer. Then I could work with you for free."

Katie tried to remonstrate, "Maisie, I don't know anything about farms."

"You could learn. Nanna said you're really clever." Jean leant forward and held the two of them. "Come on you two, we'll be alright. God will find a way, I'm sure. We've found each other, here and now. We still have some choices left. They can take the farm, but we should be thankful. We have our home, Maisie. Katie will always have Liza's inheritance, her family's legacy to live on. And, we have each other."

"But I want it to stay like this. I want all the chickens back. I want Katie to stay."

Jean held Maisie's face now and spoke gently but directly, "And as I told you before, adults have to make their own choices. If you love somebody, you must love everything about them and, sometimes, you have to let them go. We can't always have what we want."

*

Katie made her way out to look in on Acorn. Mr. Stokes, the church warden, had kindly agreed to take Daisy and her litter. At least until the puppies were old enough to be separated from their mum. Katie looked down at the little family all huddled together. Mother and babies. Daisy was feeding them, doing what was natural, what was right. Perhaps, Katie reflected, she hadn't given her own mother enough credit for what she'd done. For bringing her up, largely alone. Instead of chiding her mother for her vulnerabilities, perhaps she'd be better off thinking about the sacrifices she'd made to ensure that Katie had had such a happy childhood. What responsibilities her mother had faced in order for them both to survive and even thrive. She'd never really thought about her mother as a whole person before. She'd been too quick to judge her, dismissing her as unreliable, when in fact that had never been the case.

Perhaps, Katie mused, she needed to stop feeling sorry for herself and decide, once and for all, what it was that she did want, rather than rail against the things that she didn't.

She pulled her phone from her pocket and rang a number. She bit her lip.

"Mum?"

"Katie, darling, is everything alright?"

It felt so good to hear her mother's voice. "Have you got time for a chat?"

Katie's mother's voice softened, "Katie," there was a pause. "I can't think of single person on the planet I'd rather chat with."

As Katie wandered absently about the farmyard, closing gates and moving buckets with her foot, she relaxed into telling her mother the whole story of what had happened the previous week.

Chapter twenty-eight

Katie wandered through the High Street looking at everything with a renewed vigour. She would be living back in London this time next week and she needed time to take it all in. So she wouldn't forget. There was the sweet scent of honeysuckle in the air and, further along, she could see the row of old cottages with their pink roses climbing the walls. She had put a notice in the window of the newsagents a couple of days before and peered in to read it again now. She had handwritten it, which was such an old-fashioned way of doing things and she had struggled not to make any mistakes.

Dear Dunsford,

Firstly, I would like to thank you all for being so welcoming to me in taking over Aunt Liza's farm this past year. As you may already know Butterfly Farm has been the recipient of a Compulsory Purchase Order and as such I have had no choice but to sell the farm and land to the Highways Agency.

I really wish things could have been different.

I will be returning to London, to live in my flat, this Sunday. My flat is quite small, which means that there is a great deal of furniture and goods that I won't be able to take with me. I would like to offer these items free to anyone in the village who can make use of them. The playgroup and church committee have already taken some items but I will be putting everything else out at the farm gate (by the Butterfly Farm sign) on Saturday lunchtime for you to have a look at. Anything left after 5pm I will take and recycle. Please pop over, help yourselves and give me a wave goodbye.

Again, thank you. I have loved the time I have spent here, with you. It was indeed a very precious gift that Liza has left me.

Katie Reynolds.

A gentle breeze mixed with a light rain that morning but it didn't dampen Katie's spirit. Her mother had already begun to talk a little more about their time together in the village and Katie had even managed to get her around to talking about the ancestors they had lying up at the church. The 'Good Men' of the parish. And how there were never any references to there being 'Good Women.'

Times had changed and thank goodness for that! Her mother confessed that she had considered going back to see Liza before she died. But she'd kept putting it off because she couldn't get that "horrid time" out of her head.

"What did happen mother?"

Katie had waited.

"Not on the phone darling, not now," a pause. "But if you really do need to know, then you'd better ask Emma."

Katie was in no place to judge but she felt that her mother was starting to open up to her in a way that she never had before.

"Good morning," just the sound of his voice was enough to unsettle her.

James was standing by the doorway of the newsagents. "A penny for your thoughts."

Katie looked at this towering man and her heart raced. A sudden gust of rain swept across them and she thought how good he looked in a white shirt, jacket and jeans.

Whatever she had been thinking about had gone completely out of her head.

"Hello, I've been meaning to come over," she said.

She raised a hand to indicate what he was wearing. "You look very…"

"Stupid?"

"Not at all. I was going to say…" she thought 'gorgeous', but instead said, "smart."

"I'm going to Kent today to have a proper look at that job I told you about."

"Ah, the cider farm" a sudden feeling of sadness threatened to overwhelm her. The beginning of the end.

"That's right," he picked up the backpack at his feet and slung it over his shoulder. "With the farm going they'll start ripping up the lanes near us. The milking cows are going to be sold next month."

"No!" Katie reeled backwards. "Really? That soon?" He came forward to take hold of her arms and said, gently, "Don't trouble yourself Katie, you had no choice. It was taken out of your hands. "

So, why did she feel so bad then, so awful?

"James, if I could have kept it - perhaps sold it, or even run it…" her voice trailed off and she shook her head. "I think I would have liked to have tried, to have given it a shot."

"Katie," he bent towards her and whispered, smiling, "you were never going to be able to make that farm work on your own."

She looked at him directly, and although knowing her sudden vulnerability, said with absolute clarity, "But with help, I might have. With your help."

He looked puzzled as if she had punched him. He stood upright but she could see that he was really confused.

A car pulled up alongside them and gave a beep of its horn, startling them. James indicated the car absent-mindedly, "That's Frank. He's giving me a lift to the station."

Frank Stokes lent forward in his seat and gave Katie a cheery wave. Katie raised a hand, half-hearted.

"Timing!" James said, baldly.

"Timing!" Katie agreed.

She watched as James put his backpack in the boot before going to squeeze himself into the front passenger seat.

He didn't look at her, couldn't look at her.

And with that, the car drove off.

*

Katie didn't know what to think. She stood completely still, looking at the space he had just vacated. What on earth had just happened? Had she really opened herself up to him? Made herself vulnerable by saying that she needed his help? She didn't recognise this new spontaneity in herself. Normally, she kept such a tight rein on her emotions and now, this. She wasn't sure that she liked it, but she had to agree, it did feel … different.

She gazed down the High Street and noticed some kind of gathering further down the road. A knot of people had gathered around one of the lampposts. Probably some kind of community notice, she thought.

As she started walking over in that direction, people broke off, mummering in a disgruntled manner.

Emma Marshall was suddenly standing right in front of her.

"Are you alright, dearie?" she enquired.

"Yes, yes," Katie replied trying to shake herself up a bit. "Just, a little, well…"

"I know, I know," and with that, she gently patted her arm.

But what did Emma mean? She couldn't know about James, so what was it?

"Why don't you come in for a pot of tea? Elizabeth is here."

With that, she started ushering Katie down towards the tearoom. The wooden door swung open and an old-fashioned bell chimed to signal their arrival.

Katie didn't know who Elizabeth actually was but recognised the attractive blonde straight away. The woman who'd been talking to James that night in the pub. Henry Baker's girlfriend. She was serving behind the counter and made a fuss of Katie straight away.

"Oh, hello. I'm sorry. We haven't actually met properly have we? I'm Elizabeth, Elizabeth Marshall. Emma's daughter," she stopped herself, wiped her hands on a clean cloth and came around the counter to offer her hand. Katie shook it.

Elizabeth had a warm, open demeanour that Katie took to immediately. She chided herself for not making the effort to get to know more people in the village. Did you stop making new friends as you got older, she wondered? Perhaps in some ways that was true, though she had to admit that not having made more friends would make life easier when she did have to leave.

"I'll put some tea on, "Emma said, gesturing for Katie to sit at one of the two little bistro tables placed against the side wall.

"Cake?" Elizabeth asked before beginning a purposeful raid on the pastries housed in the cabinets. Katie put down her bag and sat down. It was a very quaint little tearoom. Along the walls were a selection of old black and white pictures which she took to be photographs of the local community taken down through the years. One such picture showed men and women at harvest time standing with Shire horses.

The photographs were all beautifully framed and displayed with a real sense of care and consideration. She looked into the faces of the people as harvest to see if she could recognise anything of herself in them.

"Lovely, aren't they? Those old photos," said Emma, appearing out of the back room with a tray filled with pots and cups.

"They are, "Katie agreed, wondering why she hadn't

come in here sooner.

Emma sat and gently placed the China cups onto their respective saucers. She took the tea cosy off the pot and gently stirred the tea. There was a gentle chink chink sound as she did this. Then she replaced the lid and the green cosy and the pair of them sat in silence.

Elizabeth brought over a large plate filled with delicious looking cakes and biscuits. Her mother inclined her head towards her to go to the door. Elizabeth seemed to understand this gesture and went immediately to the door, turned the Open sign so that it now read, Closed. The two women looked nervously at one another as Elizabeth came over and sat down.

Katie couldn't help wondering, what on earth was going on?

"I saw the notice," Elizabeth said.

Katie pouted, showing her lack of understanding. "Notice?"

"The Highways Agency. They've given notice…"

"On the lampposts of all places!" flashed Emma.

"Sorry, I'm lost," said Katie. "Notice of what?"

"That they're starting work demolishing the farm this weekend."

"Ah," said, Katie realising at last. So, this was it, then. "But why do they need to alert the village?"

"Oh, all the heavy plant stuff is going to start coming through the village now. There's going to be earthworks going on for the next nine months they say. Drilling, banging, you know the kind of thing." Emma shook her head. "I can't believe that this is all happening to us." She turned to look directly at Katie, "Can you?"

Katie shook her head, "I had no choice you know. It was a compulsory order."

"We know," Elizabeth jumped in. "James said you even went to court to try and stop it."

She touched Katie's arm in solidarity.

"I did," Katie looked back along the line of photographs. "Do you think the village will ever recover? Go back to what it once was?"

Emma grimaced as she began to pour the tea, "It might. Folk here have been around for centuries working and giving to the land. People come and go but hopefully they'll still be a small community to carry on."

Katie nodded for some milk and accepted her pink China cup.

Now seemed like as good a time as ever.

"Emma, can I ask you something? Something personal?"

Emma held up her hand. "Before you go on, does your mother know about this? That you're here to talking to me? "

Katie didn't know what to make of that. "Yes, she does. I actually spoke to her last night and she said - her exact words – 'if you want to know, you'd better ask Emma, she knows it all.'"

Emma nodded slowly. Elizabeth seemed anxious.
"And do you?" Emma said. "Want to know it all, I
mean?"

Katie phrased her response very deliberately. "Emma,
my mother has told me nothing about my family, my
christening. Nothing," she paused. "Having been
part of something here, something good, I would like
to know more about my background. A lot more."

"Well," Emma paused. Elizabeth nodded for her to
go on but still Emma continued to hesitate.

Katie blurted out, "Emma, are you my Godmother?"

Emma's eyes began to fill with tears. She sniffed
back her sadness bringing a serviette to her mouth.
"Katie, Katherine. I'm not *just* your Godmother."

Katie's back straightened.

"I'm your aunt. I'm your dad's sister."

*

For a moment, Katie thought she was going to faint.
She found herself breathing heavily, having to
concentrate just to stay upright in her chair.

"Katie?" Elizabeth said. "Are you...ok?"

Katie, wide eyed, looked from Elizabeth to Emma
and then back again, the cogs in her brain actively
beginning to whir.

"So," Katie took a gulp of her tea, her hand shaking
visibly. "If, Emma, you are...my aunt. "She looked
directly at Elizabeth, "Then, that makes you..."

"Yep, your cousin. Along with Andrew of course."

216

Katie's eyes widened. "Andrew?"

"My brother. He lives in Cheltenham."

Emma laid her hand lightly on Katie's. "You didn't know anything?"

"No," Katie spluttered. "Nothing."

She tried to gather herself before going on. "Mother said that my father was dead."

Emma, nodded sagely, "Yes, my dear, I'm sorry to say that is true. Your father died very young."

There was a long pause while each of the women reflected on this.

"Can you tell me about him?"

Emma pointed to a photograph, up on the wall. One of the more recent ones. "There he is, handsome lad."

Katie squinted at the photograph in disbelief. There was a young, tall man standing next to a vintage motorcycle. He looked very happy. And, as Katie peered closer, she noticed the woman sitting astride it, a familiar headscarf around her head.

It was her mother - very obviously her mother - beaming at the camera.

"Together?"

"Ooh, yes," Emma replied. "Very much together. They were very young of course, high school sweethearts. But it still came as something of a shock when we found out that they were planning to get married."

"You mean?"

"Yes. Your mother was pregnant, with you, my darling girl."

"But they never got married, did they? Mother says she's never been married."

Somebody tried the front door with a loud knock, a voice boomed. "Emma? You in there?"

Emma gestured to Elizabeth, "Elizabeth will you take care of Jim for me?"

Elizabeth went over to the window. After getting the man's attention, she spoke clearly through the glass. "Jim, we're just shut for an hour, ok? I'll keep your iced buns 'til later."

Jim could be heard grumbling to himself as he made off down the high street.

Elizabeth took the opportunity to brush Katie's shoulder as she returned to her seat. Emma continued.

"No, my dear, they never married. It was all ready to go ahead but then, the day before, well, the unthinkable happened."

Katie waited.

"He went into Exeter on his motorbike to meet some pals. They were going to have a couple of pints and celebrate. A bit of a stag-do, really."

Katie nodded.

"But he didn't want to stay the night in Exeter. Apparently, he didn't want to have to fork out for a hotel room. Said that the wedding was costing him enough as it was. Especially with a baby on the way."

218

She made a futile gesture in Katie's direction.

But she could see where this was going. "So he rode home?"

"He did, he did. Nobody's quite sure what happened exactly but for some reason the bike left the road and hit a tree. Over by Silverton. They think he probably died instantly."

Emma's head dropped to her chest.

Katie couldn't believe what she was hearing. Her ears were ringing and the sadness in the room was palpable.

"Who found him?" she whispered.

"Well, that was the sad thing," Emma took a deep breath. "Your mother, her family and ours, we were all waiting at the church at two o'clock. We were hoping that he'd been so drunk that maybe he'd overslept. Or was passed out in a ditch somewhere. Anything, other than the truth of the matter."

Elizabeth began to cry but Katie was past that.

She pictured her young mother, alone, pregnant and vulnerable in a church waiting for a husband who would never come. No wonder Emma had locked the door. This was almost too painful to talk about.

Emma continued. "So, soon after you were born, after the shock of it all had begun to fade, your mother decided to push herself out into the world. To find a new life for herself, and you. And who could blame her? What did a little place like Dunsford have to offer her other than memories.

219

Painful memories. Her sister, Liza, was angry, of course. She felt that your mother was turning her back on her family by taking you away. It all came to a head one night. They had a terrible argument, truly terrible. According to Liza, neither of them ever really recovered from it. But she was there that night."

"Who was? I'm sorry, what night?"

"The night you were born. Liza was there with Grandmother Reynolds, up in that farmhouse. They were the ones who brought you into the world."

"What?" Katie couldn't believe what she was hearing. "And that's where I was born? Up there?"

"That's right. On Butterfly Farm."

*

The rest of the afternoon was spent catching up on Emma's side of the family and what Katie's father had really been like. Emma recounted stories about what her father had got up to before his untimely death. Some of them were funny and some of them were sad, but they all conveyed some sense to her of the man she'd never really known.

Then, Emma went on to talk about the terrible sense of loss the whole family had experienced when Katie, at the age of six months, had been whisked away from them.

It was a lovely afternoon spent in the warm, with cups of tea and endless chatter. Katie had pretty much lost all track of time when Jim appeared, tapping on the glass and asking for his ice buns. Elizabeth had been the one to get up and pass them to him through the door.

"Well, about time, too!" he declared in a gruff tone. This reminded Katie that she had to leave and, as she got up from her chair, she couldn't help looking at the photographs lining the walls in a new light.

"So, these people, here, they're …" she paused. "They're my family too?"

"That's right," Elizabeth echoed. "We're all family, really. Let us know if there's anything else you need from us. You're bound to have questions."

She went over and unlocked the door so that Katie could slip out, but as she made to leave, Elizabeth leaned in and kissed her on the cheek.

Katie hugged each of the women in turn.

"Actually, there is one question."

Both women leaned in attentively. "Yes?"

"Now that I'm a proper member of the family … will you teach me how to make those iced bun?"

And then, once they'd all finished laughing, she left.

Chapter twenty-nine

Of course, the farm was much quieter now, but with the noise, the life had gone also.

The animals had always been the heart of the farm and now they were mostly gone. What few animals remained, they were still hoping to rehouse. But time was fast running out. Jackson the shire horse, Bill and Gruff the goats and Bella and her litter. They were all to be moved late Thursday night over to the Baker farm. They'd stay there temporarily whilst Jean tried to find them more suitable homes. A home where they might be loved and cared for. All of them were the products of the terrible mistreatment they'd received before coming here and needed to be treated with extra special care. It wouldn't do just to unload them on anyone who'd have them. They needed to be carefully placed.

Jackson had still not recovered from the loss of Spud. He pawed at the floor of his stable showing his distress, every evening remonstrating with a donkey friend who was now long gone.

Jean, Maisie and Katie sat contemplatively at the kitchen table. All the remaining kitchen implements, all the cutlery and the bowls had been boxed up. On Saturday, they would be for placed at the farm gate for the locals to sift through. Hopefully, the villagers would have read the sign Katie had put in the shop window and would know to come and help themselves. It would be easier if they did that rather than leaving it to Katie to run things round to second hand shops for recycling.

The wedding dress had been hung on the big pine cupboard.

"So," said Jean. "That was your mother's dress, then?"

"I think so," nodded Katie. She wandered over to it and lightly fingered the lace running along the neckline. "I wonder why Liza chose to keep it after all this time?"

"Hard to know," said Jean. "Perhaps, she couldn't get rid of it, knowing that it wasn't actually hers. It's more difficult with other people's things."

"True," Katie mused.

Maisie said, "I think it's very beautiful. I bet your mum looked lovely in it."

"Yes. I'm sure she did. I'll have to ask her what she wants me to do with it."

"Is that wise?" asked Jean. "Sometimes people don't want to be reminded."

Katie turned fully to look at Jean and crossed her arms. "It's all so confusing. One minute I'm pretty much all alone in the world and then suddenly I find I'm standing in the house I was born in, with an extended circle of family and friends I never even knew about."

Then, her head dropped.

"And then, it's all set to be ripped away in an instant. I don't know how I'm meant to go back to my old life and pretend that none of this ever existed."

The thought of it all was suddenly too much and she began to cry.

Maisie walked over and wrapped her arms around her. "You could just buy a house round here. Or move in with us. You could you know, couldn't she Nanna?"

Jean slowly collected up the teacups, carried them over to the sink and began to wash them.

Katie and Maisie, still locked together, began to slowly dance around the kitchen table as Maisie sang, "I'm Every Woman."

"You could you know," Jean said.

Katie replied, "I could what?"

"Come, live with us. You could always come and live with us."

Katie stopped dancing and gently stroked Maisie's hair. She looked from her to Jean.

"That is such a lovely offer. But you know, I can't. I have another life, my old life, to go back to." She picked up her water bottle and played with the lid. "In fact, I've told them I'll go into the office next Wednesday. I'll go back up to my flat Saturday. Have a couple of days to myself. I'm thinking about going part time, live off the new money and perhaps, I don't know, travel?"

Jean nodded, unconvinced. "That would be nice." She continued wiping around the sink.

Katie noticed her scepticism and brightened in response, trying to be positive. "Also, it will be good to see certain people again. I've really missed some of them."

When she thought about it for a beat though, she realised that she hadn't really. She'd missed Lucy and that was about it.

She'd miss the people here though. Really miss them. Jean, Maisie, James, the list went on.

The phone rang.

"Excuse me a moment," Katie said, moving off to one side of the kitchen.

"Lucy, is that you? Oh, how lovely to hear your voice. How are you? I was just about to ring you. How're things?"

"Oh, they're fine. More to the point: how are you? Coming to the end of your big adventure. Katie, I was just thinking - if it's alright with you - I'll come down Friday, stay over and help you clear up the last of the things."

"That's ok. But it's not as if I have to actually clean the house. They're just going to knock it down. I don't think the developers will be bothered about a bit of dust."

Katie bit her lip at the thought of it. It all sounded so callous. The old house really was going to be knocked down, actually demolished. This dining room would be gone, all thought of those special meals, Christmas, Easter, birthdays, simply erased; as would be the creaky back stairs her mother would have carried her down as a new-born and the old the fireplace that generations of her family members had gathered around. The thought of such destruction was all too real now. Too vivid.

She had to get away before it happened. Just the thought of it made her feel ill.

Lucy interrupted her. "That's one good thing anyway, but perhaps I can still help you? With the last bits and pieces we could travel back up together on Saturday if you wanted."

Katie adored Lucy. She was a very dear friend.

"That would be lovely, Lucy. That would be really lovely," she paused. "Let me know what time you're coming."

"Will do."

Katie watched out of the window as Jean and Maisie carried boxes and bags down to the farm gates on their way home. Katie had already set up a covered area for the hand-me-downs and, provided it didn't rain, thought that it might be a good idea to start moving things out sooner rather than later.

She wandered across the yard to say goodnight to Big Jackson and the other animals that nobody wanted. In the stable, Jackson lay his soft muzzle against her hand before nudging her for a carrot. She went to get him one and then stood and watched him munch his way through it. She tried to take it all in, knowing that this wouldn't be here for much longer: the smell of the hay and the sense of how still the air was. It would be a long time before she found anywhere as peaceful as this, she thought.

She wondered how James was getting on at the new cider farm and if he had thought about her. Through the hole in the corner of the roof she looked at the moon and thought: is he looking at that same moon right now? She had never been a romantic, never thought she actually had it in her, but every time she thought of him, she felt a silly, girly warmth run through her.

It felt lovely and painful all at the same time. Was this love?

She had two more days left. Two more days to enjoy the gift of the inheritance Liza had given her. Not the money but the alternative life she had been gifted. She had changed, re-evaluated, grown and there was no going back. She would have to use the money to help her align herself with the woman she was now becoming.

She patted Jackson's neck and said, "We're going to be alright, old boy. We're survivors, you and me." And with that he lent forward, nudged her side with the crown of his head while he snaffled another carrot from her pocket. She laughed out loud at the cheek of it.

*

The following morning, everything was quite damp and there was a cold nip in the air. She wandered into the kitchen and put the kettle on.

Maisie and Jean weren't in the farmyard yet, not that there was much left to do anymore but It wasn't like them to be late. She wondered where they might be. After a reassuring cup of tea, Katie decided she had waited long enough for the pair to arrive and she would have to crack on with the remaining chores. She headed out to bridle up Jackson to take him to next door's farm.

They had a barn ready for him at the Bakers and were going to keep him in the hope that the RSPCA had actually secured a place that they thought might be suitable: an animal sanctuary in Cambridge.

Katie fitted a bridle to Jackson by standing on the wooden ledge next to his stall.

She always felt a little bit nervous when she was in charge of him, he was such a big animal after all, standing nearly eighteen hands high. She was hoping that Jean would have remembered that there were still things left to do and come to help her. But whatever it was that was keeping her, it must have been important.

She led Jackson out into the yard before taking him off down the side lane, an obedient giant.

She had only seen James' father, Fred, a few times while she'd been in the village. And not at all since the day James had come and taken the cattle off the top field, about two months previously.

She caught a glimpse of the old man in the distance and straight away knew it was him. Even from far away she could tell he was very frail. His body language was awkward and twisted. He was positioned in the farmhouse doorway and manoeuvred himself through it by gripping the door frame with both hands.

When he saw her, he gave her a quick wave and she waved back.

Now, she wondered, who was going to help her settle the horse in?

"Morning Katie," he shouted over.

"Morning Fred. How are you? How you feeling?"

"You can tie the old boy up there," he said, and indicated a metal ring about ten feet along from the side of the sheds.

She led the horse over. Jackson clopping along in quiet acquiescence until she told him to stop. He trusted Katie.

Once she'd finished tying up the rope, she turned to see that Fred was now sitting in his wheelchair.

"How are you feeling?" she said, walking over.

"Oh, you know, old, but it's better than the alternative, isn't it?"

She laughed, "Yes, everything is better than that."

"I'm off to see one of those homes next week," he offered. "Yes, yes, it's a new place over the other side of Exeter. For us oldies."

He took his time, turning the wheelchair so that he was now heading back towards the kitchen. He beckoned her over.

"Are you looking forward to it?"

"I just haven't got the energy anymore, Katie," he said. "And now, with James having to work away and everything changing..."

He led her through into the kitchen where he proceeded to put the kettle on. "The milk cows will be gone by the end of the month. And then it'll all change."

He took two cups down from their respective hooks, placing them down on the work surface. "Tea?"

"Thank you."

Katie sat on one of the large pine carver chairs. She glanced around the kitchen. It was warm and charming with handmade rustic features like horseshoes on the wall and gingham cushion covers. A truly welcoming home. Photographs of the Baker boys with their dad covered the walls. Hanging centre stage, just above the fireplace was a beautiful black and white photo of Fred standing with the two sons as children. Also in the photo was a woman she took to be Fred's wife. She was kneeling down with an arm at James' waist.

"Life is going to change in a village that hasn't seen change in centuries. I'm just sad that it's my generation that will have to witness it."

"Oh, don't say that Fred. People will adapt, I'm sure."

He noticed Katie looking at the photograph.

"My wife, Elizabeth," he shook his head. "Taken from us far too soon."

Katie gave him a knowing nod.

"Yes, you're just like your father," he said plainly.

"You knew him then?"

"I did. We went to same primary school together. He was younger than me of course but, when it came to the harvest, we all had to work together. The whole school would shut for the harvest, see. He was a good man your dad. Strong lad, too, as I remember."

Katie's chest swelled with pride for a man she had never known.

"I remember when your mother was expecting you," he threw up his hands in mock alarm. "Course, nobody spoke about it back then but lots of women

231

had to rush to the church." He put a hand to his mouth and whispered conspiratorially. "Including my Elizabeth!"

Her gave a loud guffaw at the memory which turned into a long, wracking cough.

"I wish I'd known him."

"Oh, I've got some stories I can tell you about your dad. If you'd like to hear them?""

"I would like that very much, "she said.

"All right, my darling? You grab the tea and I'll get us some biscuits," and with that he popped the lid off a biscuit tin that had a picture of Lady Diana and Prince Charles on it. He rummaged inside before coming out with some digestives.

Then he began holding court. "I remember the time when your dad almost destroyed the whole potato harvest."

Katie listened intently to his stories about the man who had been her father. She found herself swept up in a sea of nostalgia for a world that she could never truly know. As she listened, she thought that this was a perfect way for her to spend one of her last days in the village.

What could be better?

But then she looked up and found herself staring at a head and shoulders shot of the adult James.

*

Katie spent the rest of the morning and most of the early afternoon listening to Fred's stories about her father.

Henry arrived later and helped her to settle Jackson into his stall. She was sure that this was the right place for him, at least until the RSPCA could find him somewhere more permanent.

He was a wonderful old character and she was going to miss him. As she stroked his neck for the last time, she reached into her pocket, more in hope than expectation, and was surprised to find a thin carrot. She gave it to him and he and he quickly scoffed it down.

"Thanks for that, Henry," she said as they left the barn. And then, before she could stop herself, she said, "Have you heard from James?"

"Just a voice note. He's definitely missing dad but says that the cider farm is actually okay. Lots of new people to meet."

Women, Katie thought, with a fresh pang of jealousy.

Chapter thirty

She was back in the feed barn on Butterfly Farm.
Trying to get to grips with a great big sweeping brush
that was actually too wide and too heavy for her to
use effectively. She was trying to brush up some of
the loose feed so that she could parcel it up for other
farms to use.

It seemed like such a waste. Funny, she'd never really
thought about consumption and waste before and
now here she was on her hands and knees lifting
animal feed into a sack.

She was actually feeling a lot more settled now about
what was to come. She would return to London on
Saturday evening with Lucy, which would give her a
couple of days to get settled back in. She could
perhaps even look at updating her work wear. At
least, she could afford to do that now.

Even as she thought about this, she couldn't help sighing. What was the point of buying another work dress? Another handbag? Another *thing*?

Before she could relax, she was going to have to check that all the legal stuff regarding the farm was in place. Perhaps, even go visit Mr. Dasher at Wilson's solicitors to check that everything regarding Liza's will had been put in place. It was, after all, over a year since the will had been read. The same day she'd fainted and had to be caught by James.

What a year this had been. She shook her head in pure disbelief.

Yes, she'd go into the office on Wednesday. Get back to what it was that she was good at. She might even think about starting up her own little law firm, working for herself. As ideas went, it wasn't beyond the bounds of possibility. She had enough money to set herself up whilst she found some new clients.

"Katie! Katie!"

It was Maisie, she was screaming at the top of her voice as she ran into the yard.

Katie could tell from her demeanour that something had to be seriously wrong. She dropped the broom and ran out into the yard. Maisie was racing towards her.

"Maisie?"

She ran straight towards Katie, throwing her arms around her.

"It's Nanna! She's ill. I think she's dying."

Katie said, "What on earth are you talking about?"

"That's why we haven't been up to help you. Nanna's head felt bad all day yesterday and now they've called an ambulance."

Katie went into automatic mode. "Quick! Let's go back and see her. We'll go in my car."

Katie had to make a quick detour into the kitchen to get her keys.

What on earth was going on?

Within minutes, they were along the lane. There was a group of people crowded around the front of the cottage talking and muttering to each other. Something was seriously wrong. An ambulance was parked further down.

Maisie was struggling for breath.

Katie tried to reassure her. "It's alright, Maisie. It's going to be alright. The doctors are here now."

As they wended their way through the crowd, they saw a lot of concerned faces with people openly speculating about what might have happened.

"Do we know?"

"Does anyone know?"

As Katie got to the front a paramedic appeared, carrying a large orange emergency bag.

"Can you step back please, madam? "

"What's going on?" Katie asked.

"Are you a relative?"

"No, no, just a good friend. "

The paramedic shook her head as if to suggest that

they couldn't reveal this information to her.

"I'm a relative," Maisie said turning to Katie for reassurance that she'd got this right. "I'm her granddaughter, aren't I Katie?"

Katie assured the paramedic that she was.

The paramedic took Maisie to one side and spoke gently to her. "Your Grandmother…"

"Nanna," Maisie corrected.

"Nanna's a bit poorly at the moment – we think something has happened inside her head so we're just going to let a doctor have a look at her. Do you want to come with us in the ambulance?"

Katie grimaced, "I'm not sure that's a good idea."

Just then there was a commotion in the hallway as they started bringing Jean out on a stretcher. Katie caught a glimpse of her. She looked grey and seemed to be unconscious. Katie's Aunt Emma was with her and she followed the stretcher out into the street. When she saw Katie, she gave her a pained look.

"What is it?" Katie whispered.

Emma grabbed hold of Katie's hands.

"They think she might have had a stroke."

"No."

"I'll go with her to the hospital. You look after Maisie."

Katie said, "Are you going to be okay?

"I'll be fine."

The crowd was parting to let the trolley through and one woman began to cry when she saw Jean lying there. It wasn't until the stretcher was being loaded into the back of the ambulance that people began to peel away, heading back to their homes.

*

Maisie and Katie sat at the farmhouse's kitchen table, both nursing a hot chocolate.
Katie had already spoken to someone at the hospital. "We'll know more in the morning," she'd been told. There was no talk of Jean having had a stroke.
It was hard to believe that this was all happening. They were sitting there, shell shocked, trying to picture Jean lying in a hospital bed. Katie reflected on how often bad things seemed to come at her in waves, often with little or no let up. Sometimes you could go for years with nothing much happening only, then, to be hit by one catastrophe after another. It was simply exhausting.
"I think we should go to bed," said Katie.
"I'm so tired." Maisie had her chin propped in her hand.
"Come on, I'll show you up to your room."
Katie took Maisie upstairs and gave her the bed that she'd previously made up for Lucy for the following night.
"Katie?" Maisie asked as she was getting undressed. "Will Nanna die?"
Katie was struck by the idea that she was suddenly

238

totally responsible for this young woman's welfare. It was a dizzying thought. She didn't actually know what was happening and felt that to lie to her now, to give her false hope, might very well have a devastating effect on her later. She was, after all, a very vulnerable girl.

Katie helped her into bed and then sat down next to her. "I don't know the answer to that, Maisie, but Nanna is strong and she's in the best possible place." Maisie seemed to accept this as this honest response that it was and shuffled down under the covers.

Katie got up and went to turn off the light.

"Katie?"

"Yep?"

"Can you leave the light on, please?"

*

The following morning at 6.30am, Katie's phone rang.

"It's Emma."

"Emma, how is she?"

"She's had a good night. A really good night."

Katie almost cried right there on the spot.

"She's awake and eating toast as we speak. They're going to be running some tests today but at the moment they think it was some kind of seizure. Perhaps some form of epilepsy that she's had for years. They think it's probably stress related, you

know, to do with losing the farm and everything."
Thank god, Katie thought. Things are good, it's
going to be alright. She poured herself a glass of
water as she heard Maisie coming down the stairs.
Maisie stood in the doorway. In her panda bear
patterned pyjamas, rubbing her eyes, she looked no
more than eight years old.

"Nanna's fine," Katie said. "She's going to be all
right."

At that, Maisie burst into tears and Katie had to put
her glass down so that she could go over and give her
a hug.

As they stood there, in the stillness of the room,
Katie realized that she could hear noises coming from
the barn. A sort of clanging sound. What could
possibly be going on out there? There was no one
out in the yard and only Gruff and Tina were left.
And they were due to be moved today. Had they
somehow managed to get into the feed barn?

Was such a thing even possible?

"Can you put the kettle on please?" she instructed
Maisie.

She slipped a cardigan on over her pyjamas before
squeezing her bare feet into her pink wellies. Then
she trundled out into the yard. Yes, the noise was
definitely coming from the feed barn.

As she got across the yard, she thought she could see
someone moving through the open doors. Moving
back and forth, almost as if they were sweeping the

floors. But who could that be? Here, helping out on her last full day at the farm?

As she got to the corner of the barn, she saw him. James.

He was standing there, brush in hand, vigorously clearing the corners of the room. It was like watching a huge machine at work, he was so bold and strong. That's when he turned and saw her. He put the brush to one side before moved steadily across in her direction.

He stopped when they were only a couple of feet apart, looking directly into her eyes.

"James, what are you doing here?"

"Henry rang me last night to tell me about Jean. I thought you might need a hand."

"Oh, James!" and with that she rushed forward, throwing her arms around him. "Thank you. Thank you, thank you for being my friend."

He pulled her tight against him and kissed her gently on the top of her head.

There was a moment where she felt completely overwhelmed. She couldn't even think straight.

And then Maisie was at the door.

"Oi! You two, get a room! Hello James," she said. "Have you come to see us? Or to stay?"

He didn't answer her but gently moved Katie to one side. He went over to Maisie and took hold of her hands.

"And how are you, my darling?"

"Haven't you heard about Nanna? She went off in an ambulance. I've had to sleep in the farmhouse.
Never slept there before. And now they're going to knock it down."
"I know, it can't have been easy for you."
"But now I want to see Nanna."
James shot a meaningful glance in Katie's direction.
She nodded in relief. "It's okay. Jean's fine, she's doing well."
James turned back to Maisie. "You hear that?
Everything's going to be alright. "

*

True to her word, Lucy arrived at the farmhouse around mid-afternoon. She'd taken a taxi from the station and arrived carrying just an overnight bag and a bottle of champagne.
"I'm here!" she squealed, raising her sunglasses and running over to embrace Katie.
Katie was, as always, thrilled to see her, "Come in.
Come in, there's so much to tell you."
The two of them made their way into the kitchen before uncorking the champagne which they preceded to pour into a couple of teacups.
"So what's been going on?" Lucy asked, enthusiastically.
"Oh, well, where to begin?"
And then Katie set off attempting to tell her the

whole story. Everything - from discovering the identity of her new family to the events surrounding her mother's ill-fated wedding - she even managed to squeeze in an update on the current state of Jean's health.

After an hour of stories, which had them both laughing and crying in equal measure, Lucy asked, "And James? Where does he fit into all this?"

"I'm not sure that I can answer that," Katie added, cryptically.

"Ah. Like that, is it?"

James had already taken Maisie down to the hospital. He was keen for her to see Jean and then rang to tell Katie it had been a very good morning. The hospital had run numerous tests and they were waiting to see what the results were. Jean had already begun a course of medication and seemed to be responding favourably to it.

Everything was looking good. Apparently, a lot of the villagers were angry at the thought that Jean had been adversely affected by the Highways Agency's looming deadline. Katie was also concerned that some of them might hold her partially responsible also as she seemed, at least from the outside, to be caving into the agency's demands.

"Let's go to that lovely little pub on your last night," Lucy said. "I like it there. You could say goodbye to a few people and have a decent drink."

Katie agreed although with some reservations. "Can't

stay late, though. Still got a few things left to do."

Emma and Katie had already agreed that Maisie would sleep in her own bed that night at Tumbledown Cottage and that Emma's daughter, Elizabeth, would come over to keep an eye on her. There was no point to her sleeping at the farm, with the contractors due to arrive the following morning.

There was a ping on Katie's phone. It was an email from the Highways Agency:

"Further to appeals and clearance from the court system, The Reynolds Farm (known as Butterfly Farm) will be transferred to the ownership of The Highways Agency. The funds will clear your bank and completion will take place on, Saturday 20th May at noon. A manager will be on site to issue the completion documentation to you by hand. Thank you for your continued cooperation."

It all felt so unreal.

They'd decided that they were going to walk to the pub but it was already getting dark when they pushed out into the yard and, as they turned onto the lane, Lucy had to look to see where she was stepping.

"What about your mother?" Lucy asked. "Have you told her you know the full story now?"

"No, there's plenty of time for us to sit down and discuss that in the future. It's not the kind of conversation I'd want to have over the phone." And I know she won't."

"I understand that" said Lucy. "What will you do

with her wedding dress? I mean, you can't just dump it."

"I really don't know."

"Such a shame, isn't it? "she said looking back on the farm buildings. "Such a shame that a beautiful place like this has to be knocked down."

"I know, it just doesn't make any sense," Katie said. "In this day and age, when we should be trying to hold on to our heritage. We need to be protecting places like this not destroying them."

As if to further make the point, as they reached the road heading back into the village, the red of the sky picked the farm out in stark profile.

"Do you know, what?" said Lucy. "I think I might try a glass of Pale Ale tonight."

The bar was quiet when they arrived and Jim Riley quickly poured them a couple of drinks.

"On the house," he said, giving Katie a knowing smile.

Katie thanked him and they took their drinks over to a small table in the corner.

Lucy said, "Do you also know, Katie, that when you said to me, 'What would you do?', I really did give it a lot of thought. Tried to think of ways that you could generate money from the farm. I put a lot of thought into it. And, you know, there's a lot of business opportunities you could still consider."

"Yeah, well, too late for that now," Katie took a sip of her drink.

"Oh, I know, I know, but well, there are lots of things that could work in a rural area like this."

"Oh, yeah? Like what?"

"Like a retreat. Like a conservation retreat. A Wellness Centre. There's so much space down here. You could stick up some wigwams or yurts and offer them some…" she caught herself then. "Well, you know. You could offer people the experience of working on an actual farm with actual animals."

"Sounds like a lot of hard work to me," Katie said, unconvinced.

"A lot of hard work, but perhaps also a lot of fun." As they sat at their table Kate said, "You know I won't be too unhappy about going back to the law, though. I am good at what I do and some of it I actually do enjoy."

"Oh, I know," said Lucy. "You are good at it but that's because you're really bright."

Katie laughed at Lucy's flagrant attempt at flattery. "Not that clever though, am I? I mean, I never got the better of that Aga!"

"How did you get on working from home anyway? You could still go off and be a digital nomad, you know. You could pretty much do that from anywhere. You could travel to Bali on your money, couldn't you? Work from there?"

"You might be right but, actually, I think that a holiday is the first thing I need."

The pub was quiet for a Friday night, Katie thought.

A couple of the regulars who'd come in had acknowledged her but they were keen to keep their distance.

Her final night in the village. Not what she had envisaged.

After the will had been read, she'd been foolish enough to think that, once she'd served her year long apprenticeship, she'd be opening a bottle of champagne keen to start enjoying her new wealth. She'd thought that selling the farm was going to be the most exciting moment of her life and that, by selling it, she'd be transformed into a wealthy heiress.

But that hadn't been how it had all turned out.

And now here she was. Brow beaten and exhausted. How was it possible for her to have been so wrong, about so many things?

Lucy reached across and touched her hand.

"Katie, you've done everything you could to save that farm. You really have."

The pair sat like that for a while, silently sipping their drinks.

"Anyway, Daniel said he's going to be coming down tomorrow. Just to make sure that the handover of contracts is done correctly. We can't afford any last-minute mishaps."

Katie raised an amused eyebrow. "Not just an excuse for him to see you then?"

"Stop it! Apparently they have to show some kind of

order. It's that that gives them permission to get access to your land. And, according to Daniel, it's not always as straightforward as everybody thinks. That's why he wants to be here: to make sure they get everything right."

"But, even if they don't," Katie protested. "Aren't we just putting off the inevitable? Haven't we tried just about everything with all those appeals?"

"It's not how many times you get knocked down, it's how many times you get back up again."

"We're not getting back up this time though, are we?" she finished her drink. "Come on, let's get home. I want to find out what shape Jean's in before we go to bed. I've got a big day tomorrow. I've got to make sure I get rid of everything at the gate. I'm hoping a lot of people come up and pick up some bits and pieces or we're going to have to do quite a lot of recycling runs. And then hand over the keys. That huge set of keys!"

The gravity of what was happening suddenly hit her and she put her head in her hands.

"Not that they're going to need keys once the door's been smashed in."

Lucy came round the table and helped her on with her coat.

As they left Jim Riley gave them a last wave goodbye. "Good luck, Katie," he shouted. "We'll see you in the morning."

"Oh," she said, surprised. "Why? Are you coming

up, then?"

"Yes! Yes, of course. "

"OK. There's lots of bits up there. Some good stuff."

He looked puzzled.

Katie and her best friend wandered home arm in arm for the final night.

Past Tumbledown Cottage where Maisie was now tucked up in bed with Cousin Elizabeth protecting her.

Home to Butterfly Farm, for one more night.

Chapter thirty-one

Katie woke before dawn on the final morning.
Saturday.

She dressed quietly so as not to disturb Lucy and made her way down to the kitchen.

She peered out through the kitchen door. The air was very still. The sun was just rising.

She put on her coat and - for the final time - her well-worn wellies and set off to walk the perimeter of the farm for one last time.

She would have to try and remember things as they were on this particularly beautiful morning. She could see her breath forming in front of her face as she walked around the left-hand side of the farm and past the pig pens. The shiny metal roofs of the individual pens acted like mirrors so that the whole place seemed to glow.

Then she found herself wondering where Lollipop and Wilbur might be waking up today.

In an ideal world they'd all still be together. The sheep, the lambs, Pickles the pony, Jackson, Spud and all the others just living, happily together. Like it used to be. Of course, she'd been so preoccupied with her own life then that she hadn't realized what wonderfully happy times they were.

But wasn't that always the way?

She took her time walking out towards the top of the farm. The birds were already up and about, excited about their day. She hoped that once she returned to London, she wouldn't suddenly forget all about them. How to tell them apart based solely upon their song patterns.

It was really quite a skill that she'd acquired there. There was a distinct, fresh smell to the air and along with the quality of the light, it made for quite an overwhelming experience. Something that would live long in the memory.

She was also relieved that it wasn't raining. The rain usually made her feel miserable, particularly on a weekend. But that wasn't the case today.   It was starting to look as though it was going to be a glorious weekend.

A dog was barking off in the distance, somewhere over on the other side of the valley and she found herself thinking about Jess and her babies. How was

Acorn doing?

The light bounced off the church steeple across the way in Holcot.

She'd been walking for about forty minutes, admiring the hedgerow which she'd worked so hard to tame and then maintain, when she suddenly remembered her guest. She'd been out for quite a long time and Lucy would no doubt be up and about by now. Before she went back, her eyes raked back and forth, trying to spot the gap in the hedgerow where the digger driver had broken through. Where she and James had first talked openly to one another.

Then she wrapped her coat tightly around herself and made her way back to the farmhouse.

On the way, she passed the barn with its broken roof, the hen house, the llama fields. All the different areas which had gone to make Butterfly Farm so unique. So full of life.

As she entered the kitchen, she found that Lucy was rustling up some food.

"Two children's boxes of corn flakes and half a pint of milk," she said. "Come on, Katie. You've got to eat something. It's going to be a busy day."

Katie hung her coat on the back of the door. Then she helped herself to a bowl and a spoon.

"Gourmet!" she said, as she settled down to eat her cornflakes. "I think we might as well move everything into the kitchen now, don't you think? Just to make sure we don't forget anything?"

"Yes, I think that's a really good idea," Lucy said. "Let's be completely ready. Get some control back. Leave the place with a bit of Lucy."

Then she realized what she'd said, punning on her own name, and they both laughed.

As they sat there, munching on their cornflakes whilst discussing the best place to buy sourdough bread in London, the doorbell went.

The front doorbell.

Never good, she thought. Always something official. Lucy nodded. She showed that she understood that this was a significant moment by scooping up the breakfast things and depositing them in the sink.

Katie went and stood by the front door. She knew that it was likely to be something to do with the order that day. And sure enough, when she opened it, there he was Mr. Rothman.

"Good morning Miss Reynolds, beautiful morning."

"Mr. Rothman," she was in no mood for niceties. "I see you've come in person."

"That's right," he said slowly before continuing in a smug manner. "Just to let you know that we'll be starting work today. Please make sure that you take everything you require from the property as you won't be able to return and it will become a Health and Safety risk area."

She was startled by his abrupt manner.

"Yes, but you won't be starting work today, will you? Not on the first day."

253

"I think you'll find that the land actually does now belong to the Highways Agency."

"I know technically, but who's going to start work on a Saturday?" she said, incredulously.

Mr. Rothman went to move past her into the house but Katie blocked his path by shooting out her arm.

"I beg your pardon. What do you think you're doing?"

"Well, I just assumed that now that…"

"You should assume nothing, Mr. Rothman. Because until midday today, when I am served that order, this house is still my home. And you are not welcome inside."

He looked along the hallway. Apart from a couple of forlorn boxes, the place was bare.

"Your home?" he guffawed. "Well, Miss Reynolds, if that's how you want to play it, then be my guest. I'll see you by the gate. At midday. "

And with that, he turned and walked back to the yard. He pulled out his phone and speaking loud enough for Katie to hear said, "Right, Jimmy. Line them up. We start at midday."

*

Half an hour later, Katie and Lucy were dressed and ready. Katie had on a more sophisticated outfit than usual, a feminine Zimmermann yellow dress and some Blahnik flat shoes. She hadn't worn either in a year. It felt very alien to her now, to actually be wearing girls' clothes.

254

James arrived at the back door with Maisie. He made an appreciative nod at her dress.

"Lovely!" he said quietly. Katie blushed.

He and Maisie helped them to move the final boxes out to the farmyard gate.

As they piled things up on one of the tables, Katie brushed James' hand.

"Would it be stealing?" she asked.

He looked confused.

She explained, "To actually keep the 'Butterfly Farm' sign?"

"Where are you going to put that in your little London flat?" he seemed amused.

"Well, I thought, perhaps…" she poked his chest gently, flirtatiously. "I thought perhaps you could keep it on your farm for now. So that when I come to visit…"

"If you come to visit," he grimaced, recognizing the challenges of living so far apart.

They stood in silence, regarding one another.

"Come on," he said. "You get these final bits and pieces sorted and I'll carry the sign over to my Dad's.

He went behind the sign and started to heave it backwards and forwards in a bid to loosen the posts. Quicker than Katie could have imagined, he managed to free the sign from the ground before hefting it over his shoulder. With a tip of his cap, he set off across Hackhurst Lane heading towards his father's farm.

255

She couldn't fail but be impressed by such a display of pure, brute strength and she gave an appreciative sigh in his wake. Then she looked down forlornly at where the sign had stood.

Just then a car appeared, pulling into the lane. It was Daniel Beardsley. He parked a good way up the lane and then got out. She gave him a little wave, wondering why he was parking all the way up there. Then she realized. He was thinking about the contractors and their vehicles.

Katie hadn't given it a thought until now but she was going to have to move her car off the driveway before everyone arrived at twelve.

Lucy plonked a box down on one of the tables.

"I love these egg cups," she said, extricating one in the shape of a chicken. "Can I keep them?"

"Be my guest."

Then she watched as Lucy carried one over to Daniel. He seemed a little taken aback by his new present but he accepted it before giving Lucy a huge hug.

"For our first house," Lucy said, and Katie's eyes widened in delight as the pair kissed. A fond, loving kiss.

Katie couldn't help thinking about James. If only time had been on their side, things might have been very different.

Very different indeed.

"They're coming!" shouted Maisie, excitedly. "They're coming!"

"They must be coming for all this stuff?" Katie peered down the lane.

"No," squealed Maisie. "It's the whole village! The whole village is coming."

Like a wave moving towards her, Katie could make out at least a hundred people emerging from the top of the lane. And with them came a rush of excitement, a swell of defiant voices and amongst them, Katie saw several placards.

'Save our village!' 'Save our countryside!' 'No more cars.'

What on earth was happening?

"They're here to save the farm," shouted Maisie.

*

People gathered around Katie, jostling for position as they tried to get near her.

They were smiling and chanting, "Save Butterfly Farm, Save Butterfly Farm" over and over.

They were all clearly enjoying the excitement of the big event. All the familiar faces from the village were there but there also lots of people Katie had never even seen, let alone spoken to.

Jim Riley, from the pub was carrying a placard that read "No cars, No way." Her cousin, Elizabeth Marshall, clapped and cheered loudly. She pointed to the young man standing next to her and mouthed, "Cousin Andrew."

Henry Baker was there too. He'd wheeled his father over in a wheelchair and was now helping him stand. Even Hugh, the vicar, was there. He was carrying a sign that said, "Save Us," which looked like it might have been appropriated from somewhere in the church.

After a while they started to settle down a bit and, eventually, an uneasy quiet descended.

"I don't understand," Katie said. "What are you all doing here?"

Hugh stepped forward.

"Jean taking ill was the last straw. This village has been pushed too far. We may be old fashioned, but we're still up for a fight."

This was met with a roar of approval, as he turned to the crowd and said, "I would rather walk with a friend in the dark, than alone in the light."

A few people nodded at this, though there were just as many people who looked baffled as to what this might actually mean.

Katie, for her part, was riven with fresh doubts. This sudden show of support should have given her a new sense of purpose but, instead, all she could think about were the opportunities she'd missed. Perhaps if she'd managed to get her act together right at the start, then she might have been able to turn this whole thing around.

Only, that hadn't happened.

"It's too late," she whispered.

At the back, someone urged her to speak up.

"There's nothing else we can do," she said with greater strength.

There was an uncomfortable silence. James suddenly appeared out of the crowd. He came over to stand beside her, his arm at her waist.

The crowd kept surging forward although nobody quite knew what to do or say.

"Yeah, she's right!" a voice came from the back.

The crowd turned to see who was speaking and then, after much pushing and shoving, Mr. Rothman appeared clutching a bright red folder.

"Good morning, everyone," he spoke loudly with a hint of sarcasm. "Glad to see that you could all make it. I'm here today to make a formal presentation to Miss Reynolds in front of the whole village. Because I'm sure you'll all be delighted to hear that she looks set to earn a very pretty penny from the sale of this land."

He pressed the red folder into Katie's hands.

"So, here it is," he said. "What we've all been waiting for: the final notice to quit." conjugating

She started to open it but before she got the chance, Lucy took it straight off her and gave it to Daniel.

"Let me have a look at this," he said, quietly, but with a certain grim resignation. He went back behind the gate, flipped the folder open and began scanning the contents.

"You'll find it's all in order," Mr. Rothman asserted

confidently.

At that, the crowd started booing in unison.

"If you don't disperse," he shouted over them. "I'll be calling in the police. We will be starting work immediately. You need to remove yourselves from this access area. Failure to do so may result in prosecution."

And then, with that, he shuffled off further down the lane and took out his phone. He spoke earnestly into it, looking up every now and then in an effort to judge the mood of the assembled crowd.

Katie's world seemed to be turning in slow motion. Then there was another commotion from further up the lane.

Had the police arrived already?

Had Rothman brought them with him? Was that it? Had they all just been waiting on his signal?

It didn't seem fair.

But then, she realized her mistake. It wasn't the police at all.

It was Mr. Carruthers. Lovely, lovely Mr. Carruthers. He'd obviously come to say his goodbyes. The crowd started to part in order to let him through. But then, when Katie looked across, she realized that he was being followed by a car. It was all very confusing.

"Hello," he said, quite unassumingly. "I know that this may be a bad time, but have you got a moment?" He held out a small cardboard box.

Katie looked at it and smiled, "If you could just give me a minute …"

Mr. Carruthers nodded and moved across to where Daniel was standing. The two of them began talking in earnest.

Which was when she saw who was in the car.

Katie couldn't believe her eyes. It took a moment to realize who it was getting out of the back seat.

And now she was walking towards Katie, giving her a reassuring smile.

"Mother? Oh mother!" she cried wrapping her in her arms.

Chapter thirty-two

In the distance, there was a loud thump, thump sound, a booming bass note. The sound of heavy machinery on the move.

Katie couldn't quite make out where it was coming from but in her heart she knew. Knew that this was the end game playing out.

She held her mother's face in her hands and gently and kissed her on the cheek.

"I'm so glad you've come. We've got so much to talk about."

Emma stood next to her mother and squeezed the older woman's hand. There was clearly an unspoken bond between these two women which Katie was seeing now for the first time.

"I'm here for you now, darling," her mother said,

pulling Emma into her - the sister-in-law that never was. She then went on, "We're all here for you, Katie."

"Katie!" James said. "I think they're here."

Katie moved back behind the gate, onto the farm side. But then she found she couldn't see and had to climb up onto the gate in order to look over the heads of the crowd.

She could see giant earth moving trucks massing in the distance.

As soon as she saw it, the crowd saw it too and a deathly hush descended, broken only by the dull beat of the approaching machinery.

Katie had to raise her voice in order to be heard.

"Hello, everyone. Over here!" she waved at them as they turned back in her direction. "Before they get here, I just want to say…"

Then she had to stop as her emotions threatened to get the better of her.

"I just want to say: thank you. Thank you to everyone." She looked from face to face. Most had lowered their placards by now and were starting to look dejected.

"When I first came to the village, I was lucky enough to meet two very special individuals."

She looked down at Maisie who beamed up at her.

"For the rest, I was reliant on the kindness of strangers. Only it turned out that these weren't strangers at all. In fact, a few of them were members of my own, long-lost family." She looked then at Emma, her cousins and her mother.

She reached over and laid her hand on James' shoulder. Only, when he looked up, he had tears in his eyes. He quickly looked away. This was proving to be tough on all of them.

"It is with great sadness that I have to concede that the farm is lost. I wish I could have saved it, but in the end that decision was out of my hands. The fate of the village, though, isn't set. Yes, it's going to be a challenging time for everybody and there will have to be changes. But you will adapt and you will move forward. I'll be donating a percentage of what I make on the sale of the farm to the church and the local community. I'm sorry that things didn't work out – really sorry – but I will come back and visit as often as I can. Because now, I have family here."

Hugh and Jim Riley nodded their appreciation and Hugh put his hands together in a 'thank you' gesture. A police car pulled into the lane with sirens wailing but they couldn't get very far because of all the people standing about. The car stopped in the middle of the road and two officers got out.

It was time to move on.

"Thank you all again for coming today. I think it was Oscar Wilde who said that some people know the cost of everything and the value of nothing."

"Actually," Maisie said, with a serious face. "I think that was Pocahontas."

"But we know the value of friendship and the value of family. And, because of that, we'll always be rich." As if on cue, there was a huge cracking sound from over on their left as two bulldozers burst through the hedgerow. This was the same field where the llamas had been kept and Katie was relieved that the animals were no longer there. The roar from their engines would have startled the llamas half to death.

She'd expected the bulldozers to stop at the far end having made their point but instead they just kept right on coming as if making a beeline for the farm itself. Luckily, their route was blocked by the stables, not that they were going to let that stop them. The lead vehicle raised its basket about four feet off the ground as it began its advance on the building.

There was a solid crunch as the front of the basket met the red brick of the wall and for a short while it seemed as if the building might hold. The stable block, though it had been built over a half a century ago, was still strong and sturdy. But then she saw that the roof was starting to buckle, causing the guttering on Katie's side to simply fall away.

She found that she couldn't look away. It was other worldly to watch as the stables, which seemed to have been there forever, started to tilt away from them. Then the engine note of the bulldozer changed and she started to wonder whether the driver might be having second thoughts because he seemed to be reversing.

Only, he wasn't having second thoughts. He knew that the terrain here was on his side due to the slight downward incline of the field. By reversing the bulldozer, he was giving himself more of a run up, so that now he could come at the stable wall from a different angle. Then, once he was in position, he came forward, slow and menacing and head on.

The driver must have spotted a weakness in the wall because as soon as he struck it, the whole top of the building jerked forwards before crashing down. As the other three walls collapsed, they threw up a huge cloud of dust and it was only when that started to clear that Katie realized that the stable block was completely gone.

Her car was parked on this side of the fence and, when she looked, she saw that a falling piece of masonry had landed on its roof. It was overwhelmingly destructive, and so awful to see.

Suddenly, one of the older men - who turned out to be Frank Stokes, the church warden – crossed the lane and opened the gate shouting, "What are you doing? You're going to have to stop that, now!"

It looked like he was intending to confront the driver of the bulldozer but the senior police officer had other ideas. She motioned for the younger officer to go and restrain Frank. The young man approached him from behind, but Frank was stronger than he looked and he had the advantage that he was wearing wellies. This proved to be the deciding factor on such muddy ground. As the pair of them wrestled for an advantage, the young police officer lost his footing. As he went down, his helmet came off and the crowd jeered.

There was a change in the note of the machinery noise and a huge construction crane appeared through the gap in the hedgerow. It was only as it came closer that Katie saw that it came equipped with its own wrecking ball. As she watched, the crane came down the field, following virtually the same path as the two bulldozers. The sense of threat was now enormous.

They could only watch as the two officers led Frank away.

While this was happening, one of the bulldozer drivers climbed down from his cab and went to open the big double gate at the end of the llama field. It took a moment for Katie to realise what was going on but as soon as the crane started edging forward, it became clear exactly what was happening.

For all its size, the crane was narrow enough to fit through the gap. Then, all it needed to do was cross the lane and it would have easy access to the other farm buildings. Mr. Rothman hadn't been bluffing. He intended to level the site today.

As the crane moved into the lane, Katie couldn't watch. She got down from her perch, turning her head to one side only to see the action play out in the faces of her neighbours. James came around and stood behind her, holding her tight.

Then there came a very strange noise. A sort of high-pitched whine, although this wasn't a mechanical sound. In fact, it sounded like it was coming from a person. In this case, coming from Daniel Beardsley "Stop!" he was shouting "Stop! Stop!"

Katie turned to see Daniel running towards the crane driver shouting something she couldn't quite hear. He was holding his phone in the air as if trying to tell the driver something.

If he didn't watch what he was doing, he was going to get hurt.

Luckily, the driver was alert to what was happening and instantly slammed on the brakes, sending the huge wrecking ball lurching forward although the vast chain holding it in place was thick enough to do its job. The crane powered down feet away from the entrance to the yard.

The driver, still wearing his hard hat, climbed down from the cab only to be joined a few minutes later by Mr. Rothman who'd come through via the llama field. It was clear from his expression that Mr. Rothman was not happy.

After a brief conversation with the driver, he began walking towards Katie.

"Alright, what is it? What are you up to now?"

But it was Daniel who headed him off. He was clearly very excited.

"I've got the judge on the phone. We've got an

emergency desist order."

He held the phone aloft in triumph although the crowd failed to grasp what was happening.

"Give it to me," barked Rothman, extending a hand. "I'm sick of all these games."

But Daniel ignored him, marching over to the senior policewoman. "I think this will be for you."

"Hello," she said, speaking into the phone. "This is Superintendent Jones. Who is this?"

As they went on with their conversation. Everyone stood around, waiting to see what would happen next.

But Rothman was in no mood to wait. He gestured towards the drivers who were now standing in the entrance to the llama field.

"Fire them up again, boys! Let's finish what we've started."

The drivers started to disperse.

"I'm afraid that won't be possible, Mr. Rothman," said the policewoman, giving Daniel back his phone. "There's an emergency injunction just been issued that I'm obliged to observe. I'm afraid you won't be demolishing anything today."

"This is ridiculous," Rothman said. "Because of all these peasants?"

And with that, he swept his arm around the lane to take in all the villagers.

"No," said Mr. Carruthers in a shy croaky voice, stepping forward. "Because of this."

He brought out the same brown square cardboard box and held it up in front of Rothman's face. "It seems you have a chrysalis."

Mr. Rothman pulled a cynical face. Katie moved over to stand in front of Mr. Carruthers. The box he was holding was entirely unremarkable so it took a few seconds for the realization to kick in. For her to understand what he was saying.

"You mean, it's worked? The conservation plan has paid off?"

"It has."

And with that, he started to weep, stroking the box with infinite care.

"I've brought one for you to see. But be careful. It's very precious."

"Is it the only one?" Maisie asked.

"Oh, no," replied Mr. Carruthers. "You'll have a whole field of these."

As he lifted the lid cautiously and peered inside, his expression suddenly changed and his head snapped back with shock.

Katie held her breath.

"Is it dead? "

"On the contrary," he replied and held the box aloft. A magnificent blue butterfly fluttered out and up into the air.

Epilogue

That night, the pub was heaving with bodies. They spilled out onto the pavement and even into the road, drinks in hand. Everyone who had been there had a fresh perspective on the story and they were all desperate to piece together the fragments which went to make up the bigger picture.

Somebody had already ripped down the Highways Agency's notifications from the lampposts and Emma sat in a corner of the pub making origami butterflies out of them. A group of younger women, including Maisie, were leaning in, fascinated, trying to work out how to make them.

Katie and Lucy sat in the centre of the pub, smiling and nodding at those around them. Over on one side of the bar James, Daniel and Mr. Carruthers stood together trying to order a fresh round of drinks. But it looked like they were going to have to wait as Jim and his bar staff were struggling to keep up with demand.

"What now?" asked Lucy finishing the last sip of her drink. "What will you do?"

Katie took a deep breath.

At that moment Frank Stokes, who had been taken away by the police, turned up accompanied by Superintendent Jones. The pub cheered his sudden arrival.

"I got a warning!" he laughed.

As he progressed further into the pub, people reached over to clap him on the back as though he were some kind of superhero. Superintendent Jones, for her part, stayed by the door. She took in the thick press of bodies around the bar before turning her attention to Katie. And then, in a moment of acknowledgement, she raised her hand to her head and gave her a modest salute.

It was a touching moment of recognition for Katie. By the time the men returned from the bar, she was starting to feel a lot more relaxed. James offered her a glass of wine and she took it.

"So, how are things between you two?" Lucy prompted.

Katie wrinkled her nose mischievously.

"I don't know. We'll have to see how things go. One day at a time, eh?"

Her phone rang. She assumed it had to be her mother letting her know that she'd got back to

London safely. Only when she looked, it turned out to be someone else entirely.

"Excuse me a minute."

She went out into the back corridor. It was a lot quieter out there. The window at the far end was standing wide open and she welcomed the spill of fresh air after the warm fug of the main bar.

She had the number listed as coming from Wilson's solicitors.

"Mr. Dasher, how nice to hear from you. I didn't think you'd be working on a Saturday evening? Have you heard the news?"

Mr. Dasher replied, "I have and I won't keep you from your well-deserved celebrations, Miss Reynolds. Congratulations."

"Thank you. I'll be instructing the bank to return all the monies to the Highway Agency. But can I just check: I do still own the farm. Is that right?"

"Yes, that is correct. I have the deeds sitting in front of me. You are still the legal owner of Butterfly Farm."

She let out a long sigh that she hadn't realised she'd been holding.

"Excellent. So, what can I do for you, Mr. Dasher?"

"Actually, Ms. Reynolds it's what I might be able to do for you. Firstly, I'd like to apologise to you. Due to certain issues appertaining to client confidentiality, there have been certain things that I've been unable to divulge - up until now. I do hope you understand."

Somewhere in the distance, she could hear the sound of the jukebox but over and above that was the unmistakable sound of Maisie singing.

"Go on," she said, putting her finger in her other ear. "But you'll have to speak up."

"Liza, your aunt, added a codicil – an amendment to you and me – to her original will. "

What could he possibly mean? What amendment?

"If you were to keep the farm in your possession beyond the one-year mark - which you have - I was instructed to read you this, her final bequest."

"Really? What is it?"

Just then James came looking for her. When he saw that she was still on the phone, he mouthed, 'Everything alright?'

She gave him the thumbs up and he disappeared back into the pub.

"I'm afraid it's something that I need to read to you in person. I can't do it over the phone for various reasons. Can you come into our London office? Would that be convenient?"

*

Later that night after Lucy and Daniel had happily headed off to their bed and breakfast, James walked Katie back to Butterfly Farm. The villagers had already managed to retrieve most of her furniture from out by the gate and the kitchen table, two chairs and a bed had been put back where they belonged. The rest of the furniture was going to have to wait until tomorrow.

Even at night, it still came as a surprise that the stable block had gone but at least they'd been able to stop the contractors before they did any more damage. The farm might have been scarred but at least it was still standing.

As Katie slipped inside the gate, James hung back, refusing to enter.

"What now?" he said resting his forearms on the top of the gate.

When she saw that he wasn't coming in, she went straight up to him, staring him right in the face. She was a lot more combative once she had a drink.

"What now?" she seemed surprised by the question.

"Well, now we have to go and get Spud and Jackson and all the other animals and bring them back here. And then we have to find a way to turn this farm into a viable business."

He reached across and, after taking her in his arms, he pulled her to him.

"You know that this is where we nearly had our first kiss?" he said.

"I remember it well."

His face was only inches from hers.

"No plans of disappearing off in the near future?"

"No," she conceded. "What about you?"

"The Cider farm wasn't for me. Too many apples."

"You'll be telling me next that you prefer llamas."

They both laughed at this even though it wasn't the least bit funny.

And that was the moment he decided to lean in and kiss her.

A soft gentle kiss.

He lightly touched her cheek, "I've waited twenty-five years to kiss you over this gate."

"It was worth it!"

"Well," he said. "If you're going to be staying, you're going to be needing something."

He pushed off from the gate and started back down the lane, the way they'd come. While she waited for him to return, she slowly turned and gazed over at the farmhouse which was still in darkness. The angle of the moon meant that the moonlight played lightly across the red tiled roof.

This is the house, she thought. The house where I was born.

The thought resonated with her, suggesting endless possibilities.

She was determined to invite her mother to stay for longer. Perhaps then they could start to rebuild their relationship. Start having some honest conversations about everything that had happened in the past. And, from there, she thought, perhaps they could begin to heal the rift between them.

Katie was aware of James, stumbling about in the

darkness, approaching from her left. He was moving in a laboured way and seemed to be carrying something heavy. Eventually, he reached the gate, propping his burden up against it. It was only then that she saw what it was. She gave a contented sigh and turned to him.

It was the Butterfly Farm sign. It told her that she was finally home.

"Thank you," she said, taking his face in her hands and kissing it.

Then she took out the huge set of keys from her bag and headed off towards the house.

This seemed to take James by surprise.

"See you tomorrow?" he shouted.

Without looking back, Katie waved him off.

"Perhaps. But only if you're lucky."

She managed to get the front door open easily enough but once she was inside it was another matter. With all the electricity turned off, she had to feel her way through into the kitchen. Then, using the torch feature on her phone, she was able to find some candles that she'd left on the windowsill. She carried them to the table where she lit them before putting down her keys.

Only then did she allow herself to slump down into a chair.

What a truly momentous day it had been. Funny that, although she was alone again now, she didn't feel lonely anymore.

Seeing the huge set of keys in front of her, she realized that she didn't have the first idea what most of them were for, which doors they might open. She picked through them one by one trying to guess at their purpose. There were far more keys here than there were doors in the farmhouse and that got her brain whirring. She found herself wondering what other secrets Aunt Liza might have up her sleeve. This strange inheritance had already changed her life beyond all recognition and she resolved that, as soon as Spud, Jackson and the others were back home, she'd making getting up to London her very next priority.

Then, by the light from the candles, she searched through her bag until she found what she was looking for. It was the photograph that she'd taken down from the wall of Emma's cafe. It was the one that showed her grandparents with her mother and Aunt Liza as children.

She held it gently, moving her fingers lightly over the faces of her family.

"Thank you," she said out loud. "Thank you, for everything."

And with that, she blew out the candles.

THE END

A NOTE FROM GRACE

Thank you for being here. I do hope you enjoyed the story, I really enjoyed writing it. If you have a moment I would be very grateful if you would leave this new author a review? I would welcome the encouragement.

I've also written a novella for Christmas called Christmas on Butterfly Farm where you see a little more deeply into the life of all those in and around the farm at that magical time.

Again, thank you for your support.

X

Printed in Great Britain
by Amazon